BEHIND THE LIVES

By: Weylyn Benson
Edited by: Amelia Oliver

CONTENTS

Title Page	
Chapter 1	1
Chapter 2	8
Chapter 3	19
Chapter 4	28
Chapter 5	39
Chapter 6	51
Chapter 7	63
Chapter 8	76
Chapter 9	87
Chapter 10	95
Chapter 11	111
Chapter 12	120
Chapter 13	131
Chapter 14	142
Chapter 15	153
Chapter 16	167
Chapter 17	175
Chapter 18	182
Chapter 19	195

Chapter 20	207
Chapter 21	218
About The Author	225

CHAPTER 1

The sun coming in the window woke me that morning. I rolled onto my back and blinked at the ceiling finally remembering that it was Friday. I had taken today and Monday off for a four-day weekend. I smiled and checked the watch on my wrist out of habit; it read 00:12:05. My watch isn't like normal watches, granted everyone has one. However, these watches are semi-permanent and are given to you at birth. They do not tell the time, they countdown how many days, hours, and minutes you have until you meet your soulmate.

Now I've never been one for sappy romance but I took my time off this weekend specifically because I knew today was the day that I'm supposed to meet her. That way I could spend the weekend getting to know her and hopefully it would grow from there. If all else failed, at least I had a few days away from work. I swung my legs over the edge of the bed and shook the sleep from my head. I stood, stretched, and headed to the bathroom to get ready for my day. I had it all planned out. I wasn't going to be a creep and search for her. I knew that I had to be out of the house, obviously, but I wanted to have a fun productive day regardless.

After my shower and normal morning routine, I dressed in blue jeans and a simple button up shirt. I grabbed my keys, phone, and headed out the door. My first stop was my favorite coffee shop right down the street from my apartment. On a normal day I would just grab my coffee and head to work, but since I was off work, I decided I would sit on the patio and enjoy the morning.

"Morning Leo," the barista, Monica greeted me. "no suit today?"

"Nope" I replied. "Took a long weekend and hopefully it'll be a good one." I held up my left wrist showing her my watch.

"Congrats!" She said clapping her hands together. "She's a lucky woman, whoever she is. You want your usual?"

"Thanks, and yes please." I take my coffee and breakfast sandwich and head out to the patio choosing a table in the corner so I can watch the people.

I drink my coffee slowly, watching people and thinking. Of course I'm nervous about meeting my soulmate, but it's more about how she'll perceive me. I'm 6'1 fit but not muscular. I have light brown hair that I keep short and blue eyes. For the most part I'm decent looking, but I'm a nerd. I love superheroes, supernatural stories, science, and math. I'm terrible at talking to women unless I've known them for a long time. I freeze up and stumble over my words. Just because she is my soulmate doesn't necessarily mean it's going to work out right away. Or at least that's what I think.

Having finished my breakfast I head to the hardware store to pick up a few things for my apartment. After a couple hours there I go to the electronics store. I get distracted there for a while looking at the new games for my gaming console. I end up spending more than I planned there. The grocery store is the last stop and luckily I only need a few things.

I stop by my apartment to drop off my purchases before calling my friend, John, to make sure we are still on for drinks. He confirms our usual meeting place and which of our friends will be joining us. I had set this up knowing the day. I figured I would be more relaxed surrounded by friends and in a familiar place.

I made them all agree not to talk about it tonight even though they have been teasing me relentlessly for over a week. I didn't want to think about it, that way I'm not a nervous wreck counting the seconds.

I make my way to our usual bar and I'm early. I find a table in the corner with enough space for all of us and order a drink. John is the first to arrive. He is only 5'8, but much more muscular than I am, as he goes to the gym at least four times a week. We have been friends for about twelve years. He has always made it a point to stay in shape and clean cut. Tonight he is wearing jeans and a button up with a vest and tie.

"Nervous?" he asked as he sat down and ordered a beer.

"Shut up John." I said flatly. "Where's Ryan?" Ryan has been our friend since high school. The three of us have always been together it seems.

"She's coming." he replied grabbing a menu in the middle of the table. "She said she might be a little late though. You know her." I chuckled. Ryan was always late.

"Yeah I do. Who else did you say was coming?"

"Paul and Julie, though she just found out she was pregnant, so be prepared for that. Amanda, Joe, George, and Jenny. Why are all our friends couples?" He inquired as though he just realized it.

"Cause they all already met their soulmates," I said with a smirk. "how much longer you got again?" He held up his watch 126:13:32.

"Too damn long." he said bitterly. "I'm gonna be the only single one left in our group."

"Ryan's still single" I pointed out and he shrugged. "Though I don't remember how much time she has left."

"Probably less than me." I laughed.

"You'll survive" I said still looking around the bar. A few people I recognized as fellow regulars, lots of new people, and plenty of gorgeous women all wearing watches. The watches automatically release from your arm after you meet your soulmate. There's no reason to wear one that says 00:00:00 all the time after that. So any people still wearing one haven't met their soulmate yet.

"You zoning out over there?" Jenny asked me, waving a hand in front of my face. Her and George had just come up to the table without my noticing. I shook my head a little.

"Apparently I was," I say jokingly. "How are you guys?"

"We're good," George said. "We just moved in together last weekend." Neither of them had watches given they had just met about month ago. Part of me always gets tired of hearing how great these relationships are, soulmates or not, I feel like there should be some conflict.

"Congrats!" John and I said in unison.

"We're so happy together so we thought why wait?" Jenny said giggling. John and I had known George for a few years now. Jenny we just met when he did. I still hadn't formulated my opinion of her yet, but hey, as long as he's happy.

The rest of our couple friends slowly made their way in over the next half an hour. Ryan finally walked in after another half hour. She was about 5'5, thin but full figured, blonde hair, and blue eyes. I keep telling her she could model if you wanted to. She gave hugs around the table before sitting next to me.

"How you feeling?" She asked grinning and I glared back. She, of all people, knew how I was around women. Given that it took me almost a year to be comfortable around her.

"I'm fine," I said flatly. She laughed.

The next few hours were filled mostly with teasing stories about me and given it was my big night I hadn't expected anything else, and a lot of laughter. I always enjoyed when we all got together like this even when I was the source of entertainment. The bar was crowded because there was a live band playing. I had completely forgotten why we were out that night. At least for a bit.

After a few drinks nature called and I headed to the bathroom. On the way back, I glanced at the band on stage and accidently bumped into someone. I turned to apologize and all I saw was red hair and long legs disappearing into the crowd. I didn't think anything of it and continued to our table. Out of habit I glanced at my watch and stopped dead in my tracks. 00:00:00.

I felt a click and it loosened enough for me to slide it off. I stared at it for what seemed like forever before coming to my senses and realizing that the redhead I bumped into had to be my soulmate. I looked towards where she disappeared into the crowd but I couldn't see her. My eyes raked the crowd looking for anything red. I couldn't find her. I was right by the bar and stepped up on the rung of a stool to try and see above the people. Still nothing. I saw Ryan coming from our table headed towards the restrooms.

"Have you really had that much to drink?" she asked laughing at me. I jumped down from the stool.

"Ryan, did you see a lady with long red hair?" I asked loudly, an almost panic starting to set in.

"What are you--?"

"Ryan!" I grabbed her shoulders.

"No, I didn't. What the hell is going on?" She asked firmly, concern in her eyes, she saw my watch in my hand. "You met her?"

"No. I apparently bumped into her and she disappeared into the crowd before I realized what happened," I said defeated. "There's no way I could find her. I don't know her name or even what she looks like." Ryan's head tilted to the side.

"That's weird," she said, puzzled. "You would think that she realized the same thing and would come back to meet you. Maybe something happened and she had to rush off. She'll be back. It's still early, she'll come back once she realizes it. We'll wait."

"Maybe she saw what a loser I am and decided she was better off alone," I muttered. Ryan shook my shoulder.

"Stop that!" She ordered. "She'll be back and we'll wait till the bar closes if we have to! I'll wait with you. I promise."

We went back to the table and I sat down and had my eyes glued to the crowd while Ryan explained what happened. Of course, there were groans and words of encouragement, but I just nodded never taking my eyes off the crowd to see if Red came back. It would be my luck; I have one chance to meet my soulmate and she disappears before I even realize it's her. I still have my watch in my hand and I'm turning it over repeatedly.

Over the next few hours our group slowly dwindles as people head home to check on things or they have to be up early. I receive a few hugs or pats on the back until it's just me, John, and Ryan. At midnight the band quits playing and John finally leaves telling me he'll call me tomorrow. Ryan keeps her hand on my back, rubbing it occasionally. She leaves for a minute, saying she's going to go talk to the bartender. When she comes back she tells me that she left my name and number with the bartender in case Red comes back while we aren't here. I nod.

"Come on," Ryan said pulling me to my feet. "I'm taking you home."

"I can drive," I said lamely, still feeling like shit.

"I'm aware of that," she replied as she took my keys from me. "But I wanna take you home. You've had a shit night and you don't need to be alone right now. I'll take you to get your car tomorrow."

She takes my hand and leads me outside to her car, opens the passenger door for me, and I get in. She takes me back to my apartment. I go to thank her and get out, but she stops me.

"You're not getting rid of me that easily," she said and gets out too. "Come on, we're going watch some stupid movie and cuddle on the couch."

"You wouldn't be trying to take advantage of me, would you?" I can't help but joke with her.

"You wish."

We go up to my apartment and change into comfy clothes. Ryan wears my sweatpants and an old t-shirt. She turns on some slapstick style comedy movie and I make some popcorn. We both settle into the couch. About halfway through, I have a thought.

"What if I go up to the Watch Department?" I asked. The Watch Department controlled maintenance and replacements for the watches, should something happen. "I can explain what happened and maybe they could help me find her."

"But they only deal with the watches," Ryan said. "It's not like they have any control of who gets matched with who or anything. That's all destiny and it's not like there's a Department of Destiny." She laughed.

"True," I said thoughtfully, "but it might be worth a shot."

"Fair enough."

About an hour later Ryan is asleep against my shoulder. I gently slide out from under her and cover her with a blanket. I turn off the TV and head to bed.

CHAPTER 2

The next day I'm waiting at the Watch Department and have been for over an hour now. My number is 258 and they are on 200, this is worse than the DMV. I keep turning my watch over repeatedly, it is still flashing 00:00:00, almost taunting me. I had checked with the bartender when Ryan took me to get my car. Red hadn't been back, but I'm determined to find her. I'll go to that bar every night if I must.
Finally, they call my number after another hour and a half. I rush up to the counter to a tired looking older woman.

"Hi," I say sheepishly. "I have a very odd request probably. You see, my watch hit zero last night when I bumped into this girl, but I hadn't realized it did. When I realized it and turned around, she was gone. Is there any way that you guys can tell me anything about her that would help me find her? All I know is she's got red hair." The lady looked annoyed and bored at the same time but held out her hand for my watch. She scanned it and started typing quickly on her computer.

"It takes three to four weeks to get a response in the mail," she said tonelessly and handed my watch back to me. "Next!"

"Wait! That's it? I have to wait that long?"

"I just sent the request in for the information. The request has to be shipped off to the capital and processed through them and then sent to Records. That department supplies information. Once they get the information, if they have it, they send it back to the capital who then sends it back to you. So yes, three to four weeks. NEXT!" she yelled the last word and I backed away slowly, shoulders slumped.

The ride back to my apartment was like autopilot, I don't really remember much of it. Now if I don't end up finding her there's no guarantee that I'll be alone for life. There are others whose soulmates died or something else happened and they didn't end up together. But still, that's your soulmate, what's better than that? I guess there's nothing else I can do, other than wait the three to four weeks and hope they have her name or something helpful.

About two weeks later, Ryan asked me to come up to the bar after work. I didn't think much of it and agreed. I walked in after I got off and nodded at the bartender who shook his head. I've asked him the same question over the past two weeks, that I don't even have to verbalize it. Red hadn't been back in. I turned my attention to the room and spotted Ryan at a table on the far side. I headed that way and went to give her a hug and stopped cold. She didn't have her watch on anymore.

"You met him?" I asked. "When?"

"Hi Leo. I'm doing okay, thanks for asking," she said sarcastically. "Just jump right in there. Give me a hug dammit." She pulled me in, I returned her hug and we both sat down.

"So... Can I ask now?" I said with a grin.

"I met him a few days ago," she responded and put her hand up to stop my interrupting. "I didn't tell you or John because I wanted to judge it myself first. Though you are the first person I'm telling, given that we've always been close. His name is Richard, he's vegan, very environmentally friendly, he's a yoga instructor—"

"I'm gonna stop you right there," I said putting up my hands. "You're joking right?"

She looked dumbfounded. "What do you mean?"

"I've known you for what? Like 10 years or so? You hate vegans, you hate yoga, and this Rich guy just sounds like a snob."

"It's Richard. He doesn't like when people call him Rich."

"Even worse," I laughed. "He sounds like those hipster guys you and I make fun of all the time. This guy can't be your soulmate."

"Well he is," she snapped. "My watch went off and so did his when we met. I know his not really my type, but who is it if it's not him? You?"

"I'd be a better choice than him," I retort.

"The watches aren't wrong," she said with a sigh. "This is how the whole country has been for forever. Who am I to question that now?"

"I don't know," I mutter. "This all just seems wrong. This guy is someone you wouldn't even give the time of day to, but he's your soulmate? And hell, the whole thing with mine? All you have to do is send in paperwork to get the name of your soulmate? How do they know? I thought it was destiny? Seems like a bunch of bullshit if you ask me." I throw my hands up in frustration.

She reached over and squeezed my hand. "I think you're over thinking this. I think the watches must have chips or something so when they go off they know who's is nearby. Then it gets sent to the capital. It's gotta be something reasonable. There's no government conspiracy Leo. Relax."

I sighed and plastered a smile on my face. "So, when do I get to meet Richard?" I asked, hiding my frustration. There were other feelings there, yet I couldn't place them. I chalked it up to frustration of not meeting my own soulmate when I was supposed to.

"Actually," she said, checking her phone. "He should be here in about 5 minutes. I told him to give us some time to talk since you're my best friend. And you have to be nice."

"Ha! I'm always nice."

"You're so full of shit," she laughed.

I laughed too, but I was still trying to sort out my feelings at the moment. There was something there, something unfamiliar. There was frustration, some anger, irritation, but what was that other feeling? I didn't have time to figure it out as Richard had just walked up to the table. I stood and shook his hand. Probably squeezed harder than was necessary. I sized him up, he was just an inch or two shorter than me, fit but not muscular, man-bun style haircut, glasses with no lenses, and to top it all off, he had knuckle tattoos that said 'self-made.'

"I'm Richard," he said.

"Leo," I replied releasing his hand and taking my seat again. "Good to meet you."

He leaned over and kissed Ryan on the cheek before sitting down next to her. "You too. Ryan has told me a lot about you."

"I hope only the good stuff," I joke, already hating the guy.

"There's not a lot bad about you," Ryan said laughing. I can't help but grin.

I spend the next two hours or so trying to be a good friend, despite my feelings, listening to him talk mostly about himself and what he does. He constantly interrupts both Ryan and myself. I've never been more irritated with anyone in my life. Some part of me is considering punching him in the face, but I keep that part in check.

He keeps touching Ryan. I can tell that she's not comfortable enough with him yet to be ok with that. He touches her back or shoulder or face occasionally and she looks entirely uncomfortable. I catch her eye on more than one occasion and raise an eyebrow, but she shakes her head, so I keep my mouth shut. She is trying to make herself believe that he is her soulmate and I am to let her and not say anything. There's that feeling again, what is that?

"Well," Richard says after another long boring story about yoga. "I need to meditate before I go to sleep, helps clear the mind and aura. I'm going to head out. It was nice meeting you Leon." He leans down to kiss Ryan on the lips and she turns at the last minute, so he gets her cheek. Her eyes meet mine and anger rises in me for some reason. Now I really want to punch him.

"It's Leo," I say coldly. "And you, too." Richard ignores me completely and turns to Ryan.

"Call me tomorrow?" He asks and she nods. "Good night."

"Night," she says, her eyes still on mine.

I watch him walk away and out the front door before I turn and meet eyes with her again.

"What in the actual fuck?" I ask her trying to keep my voice down. "I know I'm supposed to be supportive and all that, but what the fuck? He's like a grade A douchebag. And my name is three letters. Three! It's not rocket science! I'm sorry… Are you okay?"

Ryan smiled and sighed. "No. I agree with you, completely. I don't know what to do. It's either get used to being with him or be alone the rest of my life? I'm not sure I can do either."

I leaned across the table and squeezed her hand. "If you want to try and get used to him, I will support you. But even if you don't, you know damn well you aren't gonna be alone for the rest of your life. I'm gonna be right there beside you. Hell, at this rate, I'm not gonna have a soulmate either. We can be alone together. Deal?" She laughed and nodded, squeezing my hand back.

"You know you're a great guy," She smiled at me. "Any girl would be lucky to have you. And if that bitch doesn't come back and figure that out, I will happily be alone together with you forever."

We both laughed. I felt my chest swell at her words and I enjoyed the feeling.

I squeezed her hand again, stood up and stretched. "Well," I said, putting on the most proper accent I could. "I don't know about you, but I have to meditate before I sleep." She laughed and hit me as she stood up too.

"Stop it," she said as she leaned into me and I put an arm around her as we walked toward the door. "I'm gonna try and deal with him. I mean the watches couldn't be THAT wrong, could they? Maybe he's got some hidden qualities that are good."

"Unless he's got a really big dick, I think you're shit out of luck," I say with a grin as she hit me again. "But I will support you regardless."

"Thank you for that." We reached her car, she stood on her tip toes and kissed my cheek.

"What was that for?" I ask as I feel a warmth in my chest again.

"For being a great person," she said simply. "I'll see you later."

"Bye Ry," I said as I closed her door behind her.

As I'm walking to my car, I realize that the feeling I kept feeling earlier had to be jealousy. I've heard about it, but never felt it. Why would I when I know I'm going to meet my soulmate at a set time? That was the only one that made any sense but didn't make sense as to why I was feeling it. Don't get me wrong, Ryan is a gorgeous woman, but we've been friends for years. She has her soulmate, supposedly, now and I'm still looking for mine. Maybe that's why I was feeling it. She had found her soulmate and I'm still without mine. Yes. That had to be it.

I walk into my apartment a little while later and as I turn on the light, I see a short, balding man sitting on my couch.

"Who the fuck are you?" I yell and grab the baseball bat by my door. The man stands and holds up his hands.

"Hello Leo," he says calmly. "My name is Joe Halsey. I apologize for being in your home like this, but it was the only way to ensure that we would be alone. As you can see, I'm no threat to you. You can put that down and we can talk."

I blinked a few times, trying to process what he had said. How did he know my name? How did he get in here? I slowly lower the bat but don't let it go as I walk over and sit in the chair across from the couch. He resumes his seat. I lean the bat against my leg, within reach but not overly threatening.

"Now," Joe says. "We have been watching you for some time. You were selected because we believe you would have found out on your own and possibly blown our secret. So, we decided to recruit you before that happened."

"Wait, wait, wait," I say, waving my hands. "Start at the beginning. Who's we? Why have you been watching me? What secret? Recruited for what?"

"I represent the Department of Destiny—"

I snorted. "You're kidding?"

"No," Joe said in his very calm voice. "That's what we call ourselves. Though the government mostly just refers to us as division 99, given that our existence is secret. We control who gets paired with who. Who your soulmate is. We have cameras and listening devices everywhere. We have people who monitor that everything is going according to plan. We have been watching you, because we believe that you would be a great addition to our department. You have great attention to detail and you're a good listener and observer. Exactly the candidate we are looking for."

"Wait," I say slowly, again trying to process everything he said. "You're telling me that it's all bullshit? That you guys just pick and choose who should be together? How? Just by the draw of a hat? Throwing darts at a list?"

"Most of the time, no," Joe said, his calmness starting to bother me. "We have details of each potential couple that we look at and determine who would be good together. However, sometimes it does just come down to who's left, and some people don't get the best choices. Unfortunately, we can't guarantee happiness to everyone. Such is life."

"But why? What's the point? Just to play cupid? To play God? I don't understand."

"Fertility is ultimately the answer to that. We pick couples who would be able to bear children. You wouldn't know this, but there was event that dropped our population numbers dramatically. You'll have your memories restored if you agree to join us and then you'll understand."

"My memories restored? You guys messed with my memories?"

"All of participates have their memories altered so not to interfere with the experiment."

"Participates? Experiment? Explain."

"This is an experiment. Everyone you see within a 50-mile radius is a participate of this experiment. The outside world is nothing like this. We built this in an attempt to build up our population numbers again. We try to pair people up who have genes that would produce strong offspring. Like I said, sometimes we're forced to pair whoever is left, but we can't just not pair them. We need all the numbers we can get."

"None of this real?" I leaned forward with my elbows on my knees and my face in my hands. "This is all some lab and I'm just a lab rat? Isn't there some other way to do this? Like let people live their own lives out in the real world?"

"Unfortunately, we tried that. Women were having problems carrying to term, lots of miscarriages, and stillborns. The outside world isn't a hospitable environment to carry a child let alone raise one. Those few that carried to term lost the child within two years. We built this to be a safe, comfortable environment to carry and raise children in. Production rates are over 150% compared to outside."

"So what happens to us or the children? Do we go back into the real world after so long?"

"Some do. Some get recruited, like you, to help run this experiment. It all depends on how well the memory restoration goes."

"What happens to me if I say yes? I get my memories back, but I never get to see my friends here again?"

"You'll get your memories back and you will be given access to the entire experiment. Meaning you could come in here whenever you wanted, however, you will have work you are required to do both inside and out. Also, you will be closely monitored 24/7 to ensure that you do not reveal our secrets to the participates. Any sign of you revealing our secrets you will have your memory altered again and you will be put back into the experiment. You can interact with anyone here as much or as little as you want, but you are not to interfere unless otherwise told to do so."

"And what happens if I say no?"

"Your memory will be wiped of me ever being here and you will continue to live here as you were."

"What about my 'soulmate'?" I asked using air quotes.

"Your missed connection was intentional, to see how you would react and how curious you would get. How far you would go to find out what it all really meant. As was your friend Ryan being paired with her complete opposite."

"Wait. Ryan isn't supposed to be with that douchebag?"

"She was paired with him simply to push you over the edge of curiosity, however, now that she is, she will remain paired with him."

"Why? She obviously can't stand him."

"Again, we are forced to pair some people out of necessity. She was paired to gage your reaction and everyone else is paired off already. Unless something major happens she will remain paired to him."

"That's some bullshit," I say bitterly.

"One of the downfalls to this position," Joe said almost sad, the first emotion I've seen him display. "As is you're not being with anyone from the experiment romantically, unless they are pulled from it for whatever reason."

"So, I'm to be alone for life if I say yes?"

"Not necessarily. There are women who work with us as well, you're allowed to have relationships with them if it doesn't interfere with your work. Though the options are limited, I'll admit. A relationship with someone still in the experiment is forbidden as it would get too complicated to continue to lie to them about what the world is really like and what you do and whatnot. If for whatever reason they are pulled from the program and have memories restored, then the same rules apply as fellow coworkers."

"Great," I say bitterly. This guy sounds like a walking rulebook. "So you're telling me most of my life is a lie I can have those lies revealed and reversed only if I agree to never be honest to my friends again and to work with you creating terrible relationships that aren't fair to the people in them just to repopulate the Earth. No pressure."

"You can have time to think about it if you'd like," Joe said simply.

"How much time?"

"It's Friday. How about I give you the weekend to decide? I'll expect an answer on Monday. And remember we are always watching and listening so any attempt to spill our secrets to the others and the deal is off and you get your memory wiped again."

"How could I forget?" I say sarcastically as I stand. Joe stands as well and we walk to the door.

"If you decide before Monday just yell it out. We'll hear you and I'll stop by. If not, I'll be here Monday night. Have a good weekend Leo." He said and walked out the door. I shut it and leaned against it. My mind was spinning and I couldn't control it.

"This is a dream," I said to myself. "This is all a bad dream. I'll go to bed and wake up and it'll just be a dream."

I changed and crawled into bed. Focusing my mind on Ryan instead of the insanity of the last hour of my day.

CHAPTER 3

I wake the next morning to my alarm, which I forgot to turn off from my normal work time. I groan and roll over to turn it off. My mind wanders back to Balding Joe and our conversation, I remember it all like it was real, but I'm still convinced it didn't happen. There's no way that this whole world—my world could all just be some experiment that is controlled and monitored by some balding old man.

I groan again as I get up and head to the bathroom. I switch on the light and automatically notice a sticky note on my mirror that wasn't there yesterday. I walk over and take it off the mirror. 'It wasn't a dream Leo. See you Monday. –Joe'

My first thought is wondering if he put this here last night anticipating my reaction, or if someone came into my apartment after I said it to myself and put it here. Regardless, the note was right. It wasn't a bad dream. I went to the bathroom and wandered back into my room, sitting on my bed, still holding the note.

I wasn't sure what to do. I wanted the truth, yes, but at the cost of having to lie to my friends? To Ryan? I'm not sure if that was worth it. Though if I did it, maybe I could somehow get Ryan out of that pairing, since it's obviously a terrible one. But he said I couldn't interfere unless I'm told to. Maybe I could convince them to let me or do it behind their back and just make little changes till it fixes itself. No, they would find out. I needed advice, but I normally would go to Ryan or John for advice like this, but of course I can't tell them exactly what it's about. But I could do hypothetical questions or make something up that's similar? Yeah, I'll do that.

I knew I couldn't go back to sleep, so I got dressed and headed to my coffee shop down the street. I got my normal breakfast and sat on the patio. My mind still reeling with questions both hypothetical for Ryan and John and real ones for Joe.

I called John first, asked him to meet me for lunch, told him it was just to catch up. He agreed and we set up details. I figured it was best to talk to them separately, otherwise, it would be harder to not tell them the truth.

After sitting at the coffee shop for a few hours I end up going for a walk before meeting John at the restaurant for lunch. I beat him there and get a table. Absentmindedly flipping through the menu. We come here a lot and I know what I'm getting already, but it puts my mind at ease somewhat.

"Hey buddy," I hear John say. I look up and bump fists in greeting as he sits down.

"Hey John," I reply with a smile. "Hope you're hungry, I'm buying." Why not? Money is basically pointless now.

"Sweet," he exclaimed and grabbed a menu. "How you been? Still nothing on Red?"

"Who—Oh! No, nothing yet," I catch myself. I had completely forgotten about the fake soulmate thing, for me at least. "Still waiting for their response in the mail with any info they have."

"Well, I'm sure it'll work out just fine," he said, not taking his eyes off the menu.

"Yeah," I replied. "I'm sure it will. How you been?"

"Pretty good. Just working and waiting for the countdown." He laughed and gestured to his watch. I felt a pang of guilt, knowing that he's waiting for some randomly picked girl that he might not even like. He could be missing out on someone amazing right now. I take a deep breath and let the thought pass while we order.

"You still got a while," I chuckle. "Hell, at this rate you might meet yours before I meet mine."

"That would be funny," he laughed.

"For you, maybe." We get our food and start eating in silence for a bit.

"Hey," I said. "I had a weird dream the other day and it's kind of stuck with me and I'm curious of your opinion."

"Shoot," he said, sticking fries in his mouth.

"I was in this room. It was like an interrogation room. This man was there, and he was telling me that I had been lied to my entire life. That all my friends, my family, all of us had been lied to. He said that I could be told and shown the truth, but the catch was that I wouldn't be able to tell any of my friends or family. They would be kept in the dark. I had a choice. I could either continue living the lie or I could choose the truth without telling anyone. Which would you choose?"

"Hmm," he said thoughtfully, another fry held a few inches from his face. "What would happen if you did tell somebody?"

"I'm not sure," I say, thinking fast. "But he made it sound ominous, so I'm assuming its bad."

"Did he give you a hint as to what the lie was? Like was it a big lie or was it something small?"

"He said that my entire world was a lie. Whatever that means, but it's intriguing for sure."

"Damn," he said, eating the fry finally. "That's a tough one. I would have to go with the truth, as much as it would kill me to lie to everyone, I'm curious what that truth is. It would bother more not knowing. What did you choose?"

"I have—I mean I didn't. I woke up before I had to give an answer. But part me of agrees that it would be better to know the truth. But if I ever had to lie to you or Ryan all the time? I'm not sure."

"You always have the weirdest dreams dude," he said laughing. I laughed too. The conversation was clearly over. I didn't want to push it and make him suspicious.

"I'm a weird person, what can I say?" I laughed.

The rest of lunch was filled with jokes and random stories of work or memories of our friendship. My mind was still playing our conversation over and over again. He had a point and I felt the same way. It would bother me not knowing, now that I know that I don't know. But then again, if I said no, I wouldn't know that I didn't know again. All this was making my head hurt.

After I paid our check we sat there talking for a while longer and then John had to leave. I sat there a bit longer finishing my drinking and still thinking about everything. I was about to leave as well when none other than Balding Joe sat down across from me.

"I figured you'd be listening," I said flatly, leaning back in my chair.

"Of course," Joe said as calm as ever.

"I didn't spill any secrets."

"I know. I never said you did."

"Then why are you here?" I asked not caring if I sounded rude.

"I was just checking to see if you had any other questions for me since our last meeting."

"Actually, I do," I said leaning forward again. "Can you pull anyone out of the program that you want to?"

"If we have sufficient enough reason to do so we can, yes. However, the memory restoration process can cause different effects in different people. Some people wouldn't make it through."

"What does that mean?"

"Meaning some aren't good candidates for it and it has adverse effect on them."

"What kind of adverse effects?"

"Depends on the person."

"That doesn't answer my question. Does it kill them?"

"No," he said still calm.

"Then what?" I said trying not to raise my voice. He was blatantly avoiding answering my question.

"It's complicated. Just know that we run tests on everyone we want to pull out of the program before we even offer it to them, and you have a 94.5% chance of having no adverse effects."

"What happens if I have 'adverse effects?'" I asked using air quotes again.

"We'll discuss that at a later time. Given that the chances are slim, we probably won't have to discuss it at all."

"Why are you talking around the answer? Why can't you just give me a straight answer?"

"Some answers you're not ready to hear," his tone was calm as usual, but the phrase itself sounded menacing.

"When will I be ready to hear them?"

"If you agree to the recruitment, you will hear all you need to know at an appropriate time," he said. "It varies from person to person. While you may not have any adverse effects from the memory restoration, the memories you remember can take some time to process and come to terms with."

"What will I be doing during that time?"

"You will not be allowed inside the experiment until you've taken a full psych evaluation. On average, it can take about two weeks until you're allowed back into the program. We have quarters outside of the experiment area but still inside the building where it's safe. You'll be assigned yours as soon as you're done with memory restoration."

"Was I born in the experiment? Or was I brought here?"

"You'll hear that when you're ready to hear it as well," he said. Part of me was thinking if I was born here they would have been able to tell me easily.

We sat in silence for a few minutes, while I thought about what we had discussed. Joe sat there with his fingers interlocked resting on the table. I was much more anxious and frustrated. I was of course curious about these memories that were taken from me, but was the cost worth it?

"Did you have any other questions?" Joe asked after a few more minutes.

"The only one I can think of right now is will I have the opportunity to back out? Like if for whatever reason I don't like what you guys do, what I will be doing, can it be reversed? Can I have my memory wiped again and be placed back in the experiment?"

"Yes," Joe stated. "However, realize the more you go through these memory alterations, the more risk there is of adverse effects. You may not be the same person if you try to come back here and live this life again." Again, I felt the ominous implications even in his calm tone.

I didn't say anything just stared past him, letting his words soak in. Basically, this was a one-way ticket, was my understanding.

"If there's nothing else," Joe said, standing up. "I'll be going now. I'll see you Monday unless you have more questions tomorrow, just holler." He flashed a smile and left the restaurant.

I stood up slowly and threw a few more bills on the tip for taking up so much time. The restaurant was close to the park that I remember playing at as a child. Now I was unsure if those memories were real. Still I walked towards it intending to walk around for a bit and consider all my options.

Once I saw the sun setting I realized I had lost track of time. I headed back to my car with my mind made up, but I still wanted to talk to Ryan about it. I called her as I walked back to my car. She said she had a date with Richard later, but she was free for about an hour till then. I told her to meet me at our bar for a drink and I can help her prepare for her 'date.' She laughed and agreed.

Walking into the bar I didn't even bother to look at the bartender let alone have our normal silent conversation. Now that I knew that it was all a setup, there was no point. I sat in our usual area and ordered a beer while I waited for Ryan.

She walked in moments later and I was taken aback with how beautiful she looked. She was in a red dress that came to just above her knees. It showed off her amazing legs and was just the right amount of revealing of her cleavage.

"Wow," I said when she gave me a hug. "You look stunning."

"Thanks," she said, and blushed slightly before she sat down. "I didn't want to have to rush to get ready for my date after this, so I just wore it here."

"I'm not complaining at all," I joked. "You look amazing, seriously."

"Thank you." She smiled and looked even more gorgeous. I had to shake my head a little to focus. She's my best friend. I'm just lonely.

"So where are you guys going?" I asked genuinely curious.

"That Italian place you and I went to for your birthday one year, you remember?" she answered, and I was again struck with the fact that might be a false memory.

"Yeah," I say, keeping my composure. "That place was good. Wait. He's vegan, can he eat there?"

"He picked it, so I would assume," she laughed. "Hell if I know. I know what I'm eating that's for sure."

"Salad? Isn't that the go-to first date choice for women?" I teased.

"Shut up," she said as she hit my arm. "You know I hate eating in front of people I just met. So, yes, salad is my go-to choice. Leave me alone." I laughed.

"I'm just giving you shit," I say. "There's something I wanted to ask you actually."

"Oh?"

I run through the same dream spiel that I did with John. "What would you do?"

"Hmm. That's a tough one," she said thoughtfully. "I'd have to go with finding out the truth. You know I love knowing everything I can. Besides, maybe you could find a way to tell your friends and family without getting into trouble. I mean what are they gonna do? Give you a lobotomy?" I laughed, probably more than I should have, but given that's what was implied would happen if they mess with my brain too much more.

"Probably," I say jokingly. "The guy just sounded menacing about it. Who knows, it was just a dream."

"You and your weird dreams," she said.

"I know. That's what John said too."

"You told John about it?"

"Yeah, you know I like getting feedback as to what they all mean."

"True, you do tend to read too much into dreams," she said laughing. "It's not like our whole lives are a lie. Like we're on some alien planet, or maybe Earth has basically been destroyed and we have to repopulate it. Talk about sci-fi. That would be a good movie." I choked on my drink. Coughing, I get control of myself, impressed by her accuracy on this kind of stuff.

"I'm okay," I say finally under control again. "You're right though. That would be a good sci-fi thriller."

Ryan laughed and looked at her phone. "Oh shit! I'm gonna be late. I gotta go. I'll call you later." She got up and gave me a peck on the cheek before running out the door.

I finished my beer and left a few bills on the table, before heading out myself. I went back to my apartment half expecting Balding Joe to be there but it's empty. I kick off my shoes and just lay on my back in my bed fully clothed. I have to agree with both John and Ryan. I want to know the truth. It's not like I won't be able to see them or talk to them ever again. After I get over whatever memories I get back I can still be here with them sometimes. And who knows, maybe I'll be able to get them out or at least try to make their lives better.

CHAPTER 4

The table they have me laying on is cold and metal. Definitely not built for comfort. I had made up a lie to Ryan and John, telling them I'd be away on business for probably two weeks and that I wasn't sure if I'd be able to talk to them while I was gone. Then I called for Balding Joe and agreed to the recruitment. After that they drugged me and said they didn't want me to be able to find my way back into the experiment. The full psych evaluation needed to be monitored in case something went wrong. I woke up in this room and have been poked and prodded more in the last hour than I have in my life. Well, at least in my current memory.

They have told me they need to run a few more tests before we begin the memory restoration. The only comfort I have in all this is that one of the many doctors in the room is, or was I should say, my primary care doctor in the experiment, Dr. Cooper. I guess I never thought that they would need to have doctors and other people planted in positions inside the program so they could keep up with things and the people inside. Cameras and listening devices can only do so much. Sometimes hands-on experience wins out.

Dr. Cooper reassured me that they weren't going to lobotomize me and that everything was fine. He chuckled at the reference to my conversation with Ryan. I tried to laugh but I was kind of nervous. I was never a huge fan of doctors or procedures, especially when I'm laying on a cold metal table.

"Okay," Dr. Cooper said. I don't think he was actually in charge, but given I know him, I think they let him take the lead. "We're just about ready to start the memory restoration. Now, unfortunately you have to be awake for this. Not that its very painful, but we have to go in through your eye, or rather around your eyeball, in order to take out the implant we put in. We'll give you something to relax. It's a little scary to see needles and things coming directly at your eye." He chuckled. This did not sound like a good time at all.

"We'll give you something to relax," he continued. "We'll also give you something for pain. It's not overly painful, more uncomfortable than anything. We are going to have to strap you down because any movement could cause loss of your eye or at least your eyesight in that eye. Do you understand?"

"Yes," I said, my voice shakier than I remember.

"As soon as we remove the implant memories are going to start coming back almost immediately. It can be a bit overwhelming and it will give you a headache. As soon as we get the implant out we will sedate you and move you to recovery. That way we can keep an eye on you and make sure nothing bad happens. When you wake up, as long as you're able to function properly and we see no signs of adverse effects, we'll take you to your quarters and you'll have access to our complete library database. That should be able to answer any questions you have about what you're remembering. Someone will be available to talk to about the memories as well if you need them. Questions, comments, concerns?"

"I think I'm good," I said, trying to keep my voice steady this time. At least they seem very well prepared for anything that happens, I think.

"Okay," he said, turning for a minute and then coming back around with a syringe. He inserted it into my IV that was put in earlier. "This is the pain medication and something to help relax you. We're gonna give it a minute to kick in while we strap you down and then we'll begin. Try not to move."

Dr. Cooper and the three others in the room started putting straps across all parts of my body. There were ones across my ankles, knees, hips, stomach, chest, shoulders, wrists, biceps, chin, and forehead. They really didn't want me to move, and given that I couldn't move an inch, they did a good job. I started to feel the drugs working. I felt loopy. I felt like laughing, but I couldn't laugh. I couldn't make any sound at all. It was like I was paralyzed. I wasn't sure if I was or not given I couldn't move with all the straps, but it sure felt like I was. Dr. Cooper poked my arm with something, I could see him doing it, but I couldn't feel it. When I didn't react to it, he nodded to the nurse across from him.

"Okay," he said. "The medication has kicked in and we're ready to begin. Think of a safe place and go there in your mind. We're going to take good care of you Leo. I promise."

The idea of going some place in my mind was a good idea, however when I have to keep my eyes open during this it was hard to put it into practice. They used some kind of reverse clamp to keep my eyelids open. One of the nurse's sole responsibility was to put something on my eyes every minute or so keep them moist. She was good at doing it. Every time my eyes would feel the slightest bit of dry, there she was with what I'm assuming is saline? I'm not sure. Dr. Cooper put on these glasses with magnifying glasses attached to them too. So, whatever he was looking at was super magnified I would assume. They put some kind of mask thing over my face. It wasn't complete though, it was more like wire mesh, except around my eyes. Above that was a microscope looking thing that hung over my face. There was a bright light and that's when I saw the needle coming out of it. Part of me wanted to panic and try to move out from under it, but the other part just told me to chill out. The chill part won out and I laid there not moving an inch.

I couldn't see any of the doctors or nurse around me because of the bright light, the only thing I saw was the needle and occasionally a long dropper to wet my eyes again. The needle entered in between my eye and my tear duct. I could feel the pressure of it as it pushed along side of my eye but it didn't hurt. It was just uncomfortable just as Dr. Cooper had said. It was a very weird and unnerving feeling. It slid along past my eye for what felt like forever and then it stopped sliding. I could feel movement behind my eye and that was an even weirder feeling. I assumed they were disconnecting whatever implant they had put in my brain.

After about 15 minutes or so of the disconnecting or whatever they were doing behind my eye, the needle started to slide out from beside my eye. It took just as long to come out as it did to go in. Forever. Finally, it was out of my eye, a couple more drops from eye dropper nurse while they were removing the microscope thingy and mask from my face. Then the reverse clamps came off and I could blink on my own again. They started undoing my straps and Dr. Cooper came into my line of sight again holding a tiny glass tube. Inside the tube was an almost microscopic speck That's the best I could describe it.

"This was in your brain," he said matter-of-factly. "It's a microscopic computer chip designed to block memories before a specified time period. Now that it's out you're going to start remembering things. They're gonna come all out of order and it's going to take a while to sort through them all. We're going to sedate you now, but you're only going to be out a few hours. It's mostly just to prevent your conscious mind from overloading from all the returning information. I'll be in to check on you when you wake up. Okay Leo?"

I try to nod but am not sure if I nodded or not. Regardless, the nurses are pushing something else into my IV and I start to feel super tired. I close my eyes and drift off to sleep.

*　*　*

I'm running trying to hold on to someone's hand, I don't know who, but they are slow and there's so many people around us running too. Their hand is slipping out of mine. I yell something but I don't know what it was.

I'm on a swing set, swinging higher and higher, pumping my legs, short legs, I'm young. I can feel someone pushing me when I swing back, strong hands. I know it's my father, though I can't see him. I don't know what he looks like but part of me knows he's dead.

My eyes are closed, but I'm kissing someone. I pull back and open my eyes, she's younger, older than the swing set. Middle school? We're under bleachers. She has black hair. I don't know her name nor I do know what happened to her.

My eyes are closed again. I'm blowing on something, I hear laughter. I open my eyes and I realize I was blowing out my birthday candles. The cake has five candles on it. I can see people all around me, but can't make out their faces. There is a woman next to me, curly blonde hair and a soft smile. My mother. I know that she is dead too.

I know that I wasn't born in the experiment and that the event that wiped out most of the population of the world was World War III. I don't remember details about it, but I know that's what it was called.

*　*　*

I slowly open my eyes, my head swimming with images, thoughts, and memories. I'm laying in a bed in a white room. Recovery I'm assuming. I try to sit up but my head starts pounding.

"Ow," I say.

"Yeah," I hear and look up, there's a nurse walking towards me. "It's gonna take a bit before you can make sudden movements like that. You can sit up if you want. Just take it slow."

She helped me sit up and raised the hospital bed up so I could lean against it. Once I'm sitting the way I want and my headache subsides some, I look around the room. There are eight hospital beds in the room. Four on each opposite wall of the long room. There is a desk in the corner, I'm assuming where the nurse sits. I'm the only patient in here. Lucky me, I think.

"Let me call Dr. Cooper," the nurse said, once I was settled. She walked back over to the desk and picked up the phone. I couldn't hear what she was saying but after a minute or so she hung up and walked back over to me. "I'm going to take you vitals."

"Okay," I say, she busies herself with the arm cuff for my blood pressure and I look her over. She's cute, shorter probably about 5'3, black hair tied up in a ponytail, green almost emerald colored eyes. "What's your name?"

"I'm Allison," she said still focused on taking my vitals. After she takes the arm cuff off, and she runs something over my forehead. I'm assuming for my temperature. She puts something on my finger and then takes it off after it beeps. "Okay, all your vitals are normal."

"I'm assuming that's a good thing?" I ask, more joking than serious. She laughed.

"It means you're still alive," she said. "And you don't appear to be going crazy yet." She laughed and I cocked my head to the side.

"Is that the 'adverse effects' that everyone is talking about with this procedure?" I ask, putting the pieces together. Her face flushed and she looked towards the door. Obviously, she wasn't supposed to tell me that. "I won't tell anyone you told me." She sighed.

"Having so many memories trapped in your brain and then suddenly have them all come rushing back to your conscious mind can cause people to become delirious, sometimes violent. Some of them eventually come out of it after their brain has time to process it all. Others suffer a psychotic break and don't ever recover," she said it all quickly and quietly while appearing to be fixing my pillow. Her face was right by my ear, I'm assuming because we might be overheard.

"What happens to them?" I whisper back to her.

"You don't wanna know," she said softly, I could hear the terror in her voice. "Some things—" she cut herself off when she heard footsteps behind her. Dr. Cooper walked in and Allison pulled away from me quickly.

"All vitals are normal, doctor," she said and shot me a look before heading back to the desk in the corner.

"Good," he said, "thank you, nurse. So, Leo. How are you feeling?"

"My head hurts," I say. "But mostly I have a lot of questions."

"I knew you would. Anything specific about the procedure I can answer. Others about the facility, Joe can answer for you. As for the ones about the memories and the past, you will have access to the full computer system in your quarters. Otherwise we have a counselor who can help sort through them with you as well."

"I don't have any questions about the procedure, and I feel fine other than my headache, but I'm sure that's probably normal."

"Yes, it is, unfortunately," he said. "Some things are unavoidable, but it will fade in time. Now if you're feeling up to it, Allison here can take you to your quarters." Allison stood up and smiled at me.

"I'm ready," I say shortly and swing my legs over the bed. I pause for a minute to let my headache subside some and then stand up. Allison comes to my side and puts her hand on my back to help steady me.

"If you have any issues or you think of any questions," Dr. Cooper continues. "Just give me a call on the communication system. Allison can show you how to use it." I nod simply and he leaves the room.

"He likes to hear himself talk, doesn't he?" I ask as we slowly make our way to the door, she laughed. "He wasn't that bad when he was my doctor in the experiment."

"Oh yes," she said. "He is an interesting character. You kinda just have to get used to it unfortunately. He never shuts up." We both laugh.

"So, I'm assuming the whole facility is wired with cameras and listening devices just like inside the program?" I asked when we passed a camera in the corner of the room.

"Most of it, yes," she said steering me down a long hallway. It has cement bricks for the walls and tile on the floor. The walls had been painted white, I'm assuming to make it less cave like. It reminded me of my elementary school. My real elementary school. "Bathrooms don't have either, and private quarters are only wired for sound. They try to give us some privacy in our own space at least." I laugh.

"I guess you kind of give up privacy when you work with a secret government agency," I say thoughtfully. We get in an elevator and Allison hits the button that says 'B5' and I notice that all but one of the buttons have a B followed by a number. The one that doesn't just has a G. "Are we underground?"

"Yes, the whole facility is underground," she said as the elevator stops and we walk down the same kind of hallway as before, but this one has doors on both sides about 20 feet apart running the length of the hallway. "Even the experiment area."

"I bet that took a while to build."

"Most of it was already here before the War. They just had to expand it some when they wanted to do the experiment," Allison said as we approached a door that had 513 on it. There was no handle, just a flat screen right in the middle below the number. "Put your hand on it."

I reached up and put my palm flat on the screen. It was only slightly bigger than my hand. It came to life and scanned my hand. It beeped and my name appeared at the top of it with 'Access Granted' next to it. The door clicked and Allison pushed it open.

"That was cool," I said almost in awe. The nerd in me was definitely coming out a bit. Allison laughed.

"I said the same thing when I first saw it. I'm a bit of a nerd," she said and blushed slightly.

"So am I, you're good." I smiled and she smiled back.

My quarters were only slightly bigger than one of those nice hotel rooms. There was a queen-sized bed, a desk with a computer on it, a small kitchen with a small refrigerator and a two-burner stove, a stackable washer and dryer in the corner and two doors, which I assumed were the bathroom and closet. We walked in and she turned on the main lights. The walls were the same white painted cement bricks and tile floors with a rug by the bed and a small mat in front of the sink in the kitchen. Over all, it was like an economy apartment, but it worked.

"It's not much, but it works for what you need," she said with her hand on her hips, looking around the room. I smiled.

"Hey, I was expecting a twin bed, a microwave and a bucket in the corner. So, I'm ok with this," I laugh and so does she.

"This is the communication system the doctor was talking about," she said pointing at a panel I hadn't noticed by the main door. It was a screen like the one on the door, but it was about the size of a small TV. "It's all touch screen. You can search by name or what they do. And then when you click on their name it starts a video chat. Most of the doctors and more important people have mobile devices that they can answer anywhere. The rest of us just use the one in our quarters. Depending on who you're trying to get you might have to leave a message."

I walked over to it and started typing her name. Three Allison's popped up and I turned to look at her. "How am I supposed to know which on you are?" I asked slyly. There was something oddly familiar about her, but I couldn't place it yet. She walked up next to me and clicked on the first Allison, Allison Banks. It pulled up a different screen that listed that Allison's position and other information and it had a picture of an older black woman.

"Well that's not you," I say laughing. I found the back button and clicked on the next one, Allison Sherrow. The listed position was nurse and there was a picture of the Allison I knew.

"There you go," she said going back to sit on the bed. "Now you can stalk me any time you want." I laughed and went to join her on the bed.

"This is gonna sound weird," I said slowly. "But I feel like I know you. Like I knew you before all this." Allison stood up quickly and went to the desk.

"This is your computer," she said, not looking at me. "You can use it to search through all our library files about the past and what happened. It doesn't have a lot of personal data, but it has some. You can use it to search your name and see what comes up." She obviously knew me before but didn't want to talk about it. I didn't remember enough to be able to push it further.

"I'm not even sure if Leo Parks is even my real name," I say.

"It is," she says. "That's why it showed up on the door when we came in."

"That would make sense," I smile.

"Your counselor will be by in a bit to introduce herself and talk to you a bit about the memories and whatnot," she said, still not looking at me. "Joe will be here later this evening to give you a tour of the facility. If you have any questions, you can contact either of them or Dr. Cooper."

"Can I contact you? I think you've been the most honest with me as long as I don't make you uncomfortable," I said quietly with a smile. She took a deep breath and let out a nervous laugh.

"I'm sorry," she said sitting in one of the chairs at the breakfast table near the kitchen. "I'm trying to be totally honest with you, but I don't think now's the time to talk about our past. I'll tell you that, yes, we did know each other before all this. But I think we should let you sort through your memories a little more before we have that conversation. You can call me whenever to talk about the now, for now. Fair?"

"That's fair," I say. "I'm sorry I made you uncomfortable."

"It's not your fault," she said. "This is gonna be a weird time for you in general, you were just speaking your feelings. I've seen it before, I should have expected it. This is the first time I've dealt with someone that I knew before. I didn't expect it to hit me this hard." She said all this while looking at her hands. I went to stand up to hug her or squeeze her shoulder or hand or something to comfort her, but as I did there was a knock on the door.

CHAPTER 5

Allison stood up to answer the door I had just realized there was a handle on the inside of the door. She shot me a smile, letting me know that everything was okay and then opened the door.

A small, older Hispanic woman stood there. She had to be only about 5 foot, she wore a pants suit and carried a briefcase. She looked very professional and at least 60 years old.

"Hello Allison," she said, smiling at Allison and walking in the door. "Is he all settled in?"

"I was just showing him his computer and the communications panel, Miss Anna," Allison said. "I'll leave you to it. Dr. Cooper will be wondering where I am." She smiled at me again over the counselor's head before walking out and shutting the door behind her.

"Hello, Leo," the small woman said. "My name is Anna Grimes, but you can call me Miss Anna or just Anna if you want. I'll be your counselor for as long as you need me." She walked over and sat in my desk chair, setting her briefcase on the desk. "To start we'll meet daily to talk about all those memories that I'm sure are burning your brain right about now. Later we'll only meet once a week and then we'll go from there and see how you're doing, okay?"

"Yes ma'am," I say sitting on the bed facing her. She opened her briefcase and pulled out a simple legal pad and a pen. "I expected some super advanced tablet or something." I laughed and she chuckled softly.

"I'm a simpler person. In my opinion, nothing beats a good pen and paper," she said holding it up as she did. She crossed her legs, resting the pad on her knee and clicked her pen. "Okay. Before we begin, I want you to know what we talk about stays between us. I'm the only person who has the ability to turn off the listening devices in an area for these sessions. So, not even the government gets to hear what we talk about, okay?" I nod. "Why don't you tell me what you remember so far?"

"I've been getting flashes here and there," I say looking at the floor willing myself to remember more. "There was one where I'm swinging on a swing set and my father is pushing me. I can't see him, but I know it's my father, and I know that he is dead now. Then there was one where I'm kissing a girl under the bleachers but I don't know her name or what happened to her. There's another one of me running with a crowd of people and I'm holding someone's hand. They're too slow and I'm losing them in the crowd, but I don't know who they are. And there's one of me blowing out my birthday candles and my mother is there, and I know that she is dead too. I know that I wasn't born in the experiment and I know the event was called World War III." Miss Anna is scratching away on her legal pad.

"You said that you know your father and mother are dead, how do you know that?"

"I'm not sure," I say trying to think about it. "Just when I picture my mother at my birthday or my father pushing me on the swing, I feel sadness and almost empty. I know that they're gone. That those are precious memories. That I won't see them again."

"You mentioned running in a crowd and losing someone's hand in it. Do you know what you were running to or from?"

"I remember sirens," I respond, my eyes closed, picturing it. "But not like police sirens, like tornado sirens. Maybe we're going to a tornado shelter? I'm not sure."

"Keep your eyes closed," She says calmly. "What do you see ahead of you? Can you see ahead of the people?"

"There's too many—wait, I can see between them, it looks like a hole in the ground. There's a man standing next to it holding up the door for it. He's in an army uniform and he's got some type of gun. I'm not thinking it's a tornado shelter. Wait is it a fallout shelter?" I open my eyes and look at her.

"You were correct in that the event was called World War III," she said softly. "And I can guarantee that that was a fallout shelter that you were running to. They were installed in the late 2020's throughout the country after unrest with foreign countries. What followed years later was the largest War the world had ever seen. It started in the year 2043 with simple tactics, invading other countries, infantry, casualties yes, but no where near the amount when the nuclear weapons were unleashed by both sides. It was 2049, we had more advanced warning systems, however, they learned how to trick our systems, so we had even less time. We should have had an hour notice at least to evacuate, but we ended up only having about 20 minutes.

"Trying to evacuate 325 million people into these fallout shelters in 20 minutes was impossible. We, of course, fired our nukes as well as soon as we realized they had fired theirs. 200 million people in this country alone were killed that day. Another 100 million died over the next few years from radiation or from the fallout. We're, to this day, still not sure how many people survived around the world. All we know is the surface world is still so irradiated, people live about a quarter as long as they do down here."

"What year is it now?" I asked. In the experiment I was told it was in the early 2000's, obviously because that was a good time before all this.

"It's 2122," she said. "Before you ask how that is possible given that you remember running to the fallout shelter, I will tell you. You were 16 when you made it to the fallout shelter, all of us who made it before they had to shut the doors were frozen. Cryosleep kind of thing, I'm not sure about it all, I'm not a scientist. The point is they put us to sleep, and we woke our same age years later."

"So, if I'm 25 now that means I've been awake for 9 years," I said, slowing wrapping my head around all this. "Have I been in the experiment the whole time?"

"Hold on," she said, reaching into her briefcase again and pulling out a file. I saw that it had my name on it. "'Leo Matthew Parks, born November 7, 2033, entered cryosleep unknown date year 2049, woken May 25, 2113. Placed in experiment on June 10, 2115. Removed from experiment July 29, 2122.' So, no you were in this facility for a little over two years before you went into the experiment."

"Does that file have more information than just dates in it? Does it have my parents' names? Can I see it?" I ask excitedly.

"Yes," she said. "I'm going to leave it with you when we're done. That way you have the rest of the day and most of tomorrow to look it over. I'll have to take it back to records after our appointment tomorrow."

"I'm okay with that," I said, eager to investigate the file. She placed the file on my desk out of my reach. "Can I ask you something kind of off topic?"

"Sure."

"Allison, the nurse that was in here with me when you got here," I started, unsure of how to ask. "I told her that I felt like I knew her, like before all this. She said that we did know each other before all this, but that she was going to let me sort through my memories more before we talked about it. Is there anyway of knowing how I knew her sooner than that?"

"Unfortunately, she was my patient before and I'm unable to tell you anything about your relationship with her before all of this," she said softly, she reminded me of a grandmother, she was only missing saying 'sweetie.' "I can confirm what she said. You did know each other before. She did speak about you once her memory was restored."

"So, she was in the experiment too?"

"Yes, she was. However, I feel it would be best for you to discuss that with her. I agree with her, though, that it would be best to wait till you've figured out for yourself how you two knew each other. Sometimes, when you're working on your own memories and someone tells you things that happened before, it can make it harder to sort through your own memories." I sighed.

"I thought you were going to say that." She chuckled.

"I can see that you are not the most patient person," she said lightly. "Unfortunately, the only thing that will make you able to sort through your memories is time."

"There's no super advanced machine that can sort through them for me and play them back like a movie?" I smiled, so she knew I was joking.

"That would save time," she laughed. "But no." She looked at her watch and, of course, I thought of the soulmate watches. Then remember I'm not in that experiment anymore, so hers probably tells the time. "I'm going to cut it short today, that way you'll have some time to go through that folder that you're itching to go through before Joe comes by for your tour. And just so you're aware, there's a letter in there that you wrote to yourself before you had your memory blocked." I looked at the folder anxiously while Miss Anna put her pad and pen back in her briefcase and stood up. I stood as well.

"Thank you, Miss Anna," I said kindly. "Same time tomorrow?"

"Yes, sir," she said as I opened the door for her. "Have a good rest of your day Leo."

"You, too." I shut the door behind her. As soon as the door was shut, I bounded back to my desk and sat in the chair. I took a deep breath and tried to calm myself. I opened the folder and the first thing I noticed was on the left side, paper clipped to the top of the folder, was a picture of me. Younger me, probably taken right before I went into the program. I looked skinnier and tired. I pulled that off and looked at the pages underneath it.

The first page was the one that Miss Anna had to be reading from, mostly just dates and basic information on me. I skimmed it and stopped at the bottom when I reached the 'parent's information' section.

"Mother: Carolyn Leona Parks. Born: April 17, 2004. Deceased: 2049"

"Father: Matthew Luke Parks. Born: October 15, 2001. Deceased: 2049"

I sat back in the desk chair, I was named after both my parents in a way. "Carolyn and Matthew," I said to myself. "Carolyn and Matthew." Those were my parents, I wondered what they looked like. I vaguely remember the memory of my birthday with my mother but was completely clueless about what my father looked like. I looked back at the paper and saw more.

"Sibling(s): Amanda Marie Parks. Born: October 22, 2037. Deceased: January 15, 2040"

I had a little sister. She died before the War. I wonder what happened to her. I was 6 when she died. Maybe she was at my 5th birthday party that I remember partly. I looked at the paper again and didn't see anything else. I flipped it upside down next to the picture of me.

The next page was a lot of medical verbiage, most of which I didn't understand. I flipped that one on top of the first one. The third page was a psych evaluation that was done after I was woken up. Nothing too exciting, of course devastated about my parents, but normal otherwise for a 16-year-old. Next page was an evaluation of performance, apparently, I had school during to two years I was here before I went in.

"Leo shows great aptitude for math and science. Would be great in the engineering department. He does well on school work but tends to be a bit more social than we would like. In particular with Allison. We've had to separate them on multiple occasions. I look forward to seeing what he will become if he isn't chosen for the program."

Allison! So we knew each other in here too before we went into the program. I flipped that page over with the others and grabbed the next one. This one was a disciplinary action.

"Leo Parks (17) and Allison Sherrow (16) were caught wandering the corridors after curfew. Both were apprised of the rules that state they are to remain in their dormitories after 9 PM every night. They both have already received warnings for this exact violation and were informed that this infraction would be written in their file this time."

Apparently, we were trouble makers, I thought and laughed to myself. I flipped it over like the rest and saw that the next thing in the folder was an envelope stapled to the folder with my name written on it. I detached it from the folder and flipped it to open it. It wasn't sealed, so I'm assuming it had been read. I pulled the papers out of the envelope and unfolded them.

Leo,

Writing a letter to yourself in the future is very weird, I have to tell you. They told me that when you read this you probably won't remember writing it or most of our childhood. They said that you would remember after some time, but it could take a while. So, I'll tell you a bit about it, I guess. We had a good childhood for the most part. You broke your wrist when you were 4 and it still pops if you rotate it too much. That was about the time that Mandy was born too. She had cancer and died when we were 6. After that, mom and dad had a rough time for a while. They went to counseling for years. They sent us to counseling too, though I took it better than they did I guess since I was so young myself.

School was kind of a getaway for a while. Away from mom and dad fighting all the time. I could focus on homework when I got home, or I would always have a book that I checked out in the library. We love to read, even now. We also really like math and science. I wanted to go into the engineering department, but I got picked for the experiment. Allison did too though, so hopefully we'll find our way back to each other. Oh wait. You probably don't remember her yet. Allison Sherrow is our best friend. She was also our first kiss, and I'm about 99% sure she's going to be the girl we marry. But hell, who knows with this stupid experiment now. But anyway, we met her in 5th grade, we sat behind her in math class and we would pass notes most of the class. We were also very competitive when it came to being top of the class. She was cute then and she's still cute now and I'm sure she'll still be cute when you see her again. She just understands us, and we understand her.

The day those sirens went off, that was a scary day. It was a Saturday, mom and dad had gone to the grocery store. Allison was over and we were working on a project for school. We had been told in school about what to do if the sirens went off there or at home. We were told to talk to our parents about where our closest shelter was and how to get there the fastest. And we did, dad even had us do drills to make sure we could get there in time. I always thought it was like the fire and tornado drills you do at school, you do them all the time, but you never have to use them. Anyway, they went off that Saturday and I did what dad always told me, I dropped everything and ran out the door, dragging Allison with me. She was slower than me and I lost grip on her hand at one point, I had to fight my way through the crowd to find her again. I wasn't about to go into that shelter without her.

We got into the shelter along with all the other people that were running with us, it was at that point I thought about our parents.

I realized that with my parents out to the grocery store, they might have made it into another shelter, or maybe even made it into this one. Allison's parents had died when she was little, as cold as this sounds, she lived with foster parents at the time and I don't think she cared if they made it or not. Let me just say this about her foster dad, if I was ever going to kill someone, it would be him. I started looking around at all the people trying to see if my parents had made it. I was dragging Allison along, with a tighter grip on her hand this time.

I couldn't find them, I kept telling myself that they had to have made it to another shelter by the store. But of course, with all the chaos of getting in here it's not like I could ask just anyone. I found a corner sort of away from everyone else for us to sit down and try to calm down. We were both scared, I wrapped my arms around Allison just as the first one hit. It was a loud boom far above us, given that we had about million stairs to get down here. It shook the whole shelter and the lights flickered. Allison buried her head in my chest, and she shook with how scared she was. I held her tightly, we sat there for another hour or two, through at least ten more bombs. I lost count, each one was a different distance from us too, so it was hard to keep track of. The shelter held and eventually the sounds died off. Some military people that were huddled down like the rest of us eventually got up and started directing us to different areas. There were these big rooms with hundreds of beds in rows. Allison and I found a couple in the corner and that's how we were for at least a week.

After that, they started taking families and pairs of people at a time. I found out later that was when they were freezing people, or cryo-whatever they called it. They tried to take Allison alone, but of course, I told them I had to go with her. They took us to a room, where some old guy explained that after so many nuclear bombs going off, the surface wasn't survivable any more. So, they were gonna freeze us until it was. I told him that they have to wake us together. They said that was why they were taking families together and whatnot, that way they'll be kept together. I asked if he had any contact with the other shelters and he said the shockwaves had knocked out communications. He asked us our names, birthdays, basic information.

Then they took us to a lab where they drew our blood and did some tests and we had to answer a whole bunch of questions and then they took us to this big long room with these tubes. I could see some of them already had people in them.

I gave Allison another hug and I kissed her. "I'll see you on the other side," I said to her. The next thing I knew they were waking us up and it was over 60 years later. They told us that some of the people in the tubes hadn't made it, something had gone wrong was all they said. Allison and I made it through. They said they finally had contact with the other shelters. I asked about my parents and they said they hadn't made it to a shelter. Which means they died in the explosions. I miss them still, but I hope it was quick for them and I'm glad they were together. It would have been worse if one had made it and the other didn't. Even though they had a rough time after Mandy died, they loved each other so much.

Since they woke us up, they've had us in classes. There aren't a lot of kids our age, about 10 of us. There were more younger kids than our age. Some of the people had been woken up before Allison and I and they were already working on expanding the facility for this experiment. I know the point is to test fertility in a controlled environment, but I don't understand why we can't just test fertility in our shelter. But I'm no scientist, whatever. Anyway, I have to go do more tests and things before I go into the experiment. So, I'm gonna sign off now. Haha.

>*See you around Leo,*
>
>*Leo*

I took a deep breath and read the letter again. I'm sure it was weird to write a letter to your future self, but it was weirder to read a letter from your past self that you don't remember writing. It definitely explains why I felt so close to Allison as soon as I talked to her. We were practically inseparable from the sound of it. I remember how I felt when I lost grip on her hand, now that I know it was her hand, I was terrified of losing her. Given what I said about being willing to kill her foster dad, I can think of only a couple things I would say that about. I'm hoping the bastard's dead. Though I don't think I'm going to ask her about that any time soon.

I put the letter back in the envelope and set it on the desk. I lean back in the chair again and wonder how long Allison has been out of the program. How long she has known that we were so close and not having me here with her. I wonder if she had access to viewing the experiment? Could she see me living in there never knowing her? Did she watch how close I was to Ryan and John, but not her? Of course, I wanted to ask her all of these things, but I wanted to take some time and try to remember us for myself, not what I told myself. I almost laughed at the irony of that thought. I glanced at the computer on the desk.

I leaned forward again and touched the screen. It came to life and showed only a search bar. I'm assuming that's all I had access to for now. 'Leo Parks,' I typed and hit enter. A lot of the same information the file had, mostly about being in the program. My parents and sisters' names and death dates. I clicked back on the search bar, 'Allison Sherrow.'

'Allison Elizabeth Sherrow. Born: July 17, 2034. Entered cryosleep on unknown date year 2049. Woken: May 25, 2113. Placed in experiment: June 10, 2115. Removed from experiment: December 15, 2121. Position held: Nurse. Parents: Unknown.' She had been out for almost a year before I got out. I can only imagine what it was like to not know anyone, though it's not like I know anyone. I know that I know Allison, but I don't know know her. Again, with the ironic thoughts. Of course, this doesn't have any super personal information, just basics. I would love to be able to read her letter to herself. I leaned back in my chair again, fingers interlocked behind my head, thinking about my own letter again.

* * *

I'm under the bleachers again, with the girl with black hair. She looks nervous, I put my hand on hers.

"We don't have to do this if you don't want to Allison," I hear myself say and she shook her head.

"No," she said. "I want to. I don't want to be the only girl in 7th grade who hasn't kissed a boy. And you're the only one I trust."

"Okay. I'll see you on the other side," I say, and she laughs. I lean forward and close my eyes, gently touching my lips to hers. We stay like that for a few seconds and then I pull back.

"That was…. Interesting," she said.

"That bad, huh?" I ask in mock seriousness and she laughed. "That was my first too, you know?"

"I know," she said, "How was it?"

"I liked it personally," I said. "I'm down to be your Guinea pig any day." I smiled and she laughed, as she blushed.

"You're not helping."

"Am I supposed to tell you it was terrible? My bad. The worst I've ever had," I joked, and she hit me as she laughed.

"That's not helping either. You know what, just come here," she said, and she grabbed my face pulling me to her. She kissed me again, this time harder. I slide my hand behind her head, pulling her towards me as I take the kiss deeper. It's sloppy and wet, but I enjoy it. She puts her hand on my chest and pushes me away, I pull back.

"You okay?" I asked, concerned.

"Just… I just need a minute," she said, I cock my head to the side and see that she's blushing. I can't help but start laughing and she hits me again. "You're still not helping."

"You're cute," I say and laugh again, she joins in.

CHAPTER 6

There's a knock at my door and I'm jolted awake. I shake the sleep from my head and stand up to answer the door. I pull the door open to see Balding Joe standing there. I had gotten so wrapped up in my file and then I apparently fell asleep, I had forgotten about my tour.

"Hello Leo," Joe said in his calm manner.

"Hi Joe," I say almost sarcastically.

"Ready for your tour?"

"As I'll ever be."

I step out of the door and shut it behind me. I follow Joe down the hall to the elevator.

"As I'm sure you already know, the entire facility is underground," Joe said as we entered the elevator. He hit the B2 button. "The ground level requires a key to access. That way no one accidently wanders up there. B1 is the control level, meaning for the whole facility, electricity, life support, sewage, and everything it takes to run the facility. Nothing too exciting up there, just a bunch of panels and screens. It's a pretty self-sufficient system, so there's only a few people up there to monitor it. B2 is our recreational level." The elevator stopped and the doors opened and we stepped out.

The first thing I see is that this hallway has mostly glass as walls. Though it must be plexiglass or something sturdier, because as we walked down the hallway, a basketball hit the glass as we passed. I looked in and there were about ten people on a half basketball court playing. The room across from it had what I'm assuming was racquetball, two people, a small black ball that they were hitting against the opposite wall. The next room down had a lot of chain link fences and a net hanging close to the ceiling. I realized it was a batting cage, and apparently, they weren't as confident in the sturdy glass in this room.

"As you can see, we have a lot of options to choose from," Joe said as we continued walking down the hallway. "Basketball, baseball, racquetball, weights, exercise equipment, tennis, we even have a couple bowling lanes." He gestured towards one of the far rooms, where there were indeed two bowling lanes. We reached the end of the hallway, where there was another elevator.

"This floor is open 24/7 for everyone," Joe said as the doors opened, and we entered. "Some people will be up here at 2 in the morning because they can't sleep." He hit the B3 button. "B3 is our library level."

Sure enough, the doors opened again, and the entire floor was nothing but wall to wall shelves full of books. I knew I would end up spending a lot of time on this floor.

"When this facility was first built," Joe said as we walked through the library level. "They brought copies of every book they could get their hands on. And given that the surface has been mostly destroyed, it was good that they did. This level is also 24/7 and you can bring books back to your quarters if you would like. There are chairs and couches available here as well if you'd prefer to stay here." We had reached the first elevator again, Joe hit the B15 button.

"Levels B4 to B14 are all personal quarters. They all look the same as your level. B15 is our grocery and food level."

The doors opened into what looked like a mall food court. There were a few places along the walls to get food, but the center was filled with tables and chairs. There were quite a few people in this area. I glanced around, recognizing a few people here and there, but not sure where from. I spotted Allison at a table with some other nurses, she was laughing. She glanced up and caught my eye, she looked surprised, but smiled at me. I smiled back and tried to focus on what Joe was saying and not the memory of kissing her under the bleachers.

"—there's a few choices here if you don't feel like cooking," Joe was saying. "There's no cost for anything in this facility, but you're limited obviously. This level also has our grocery shopping area." Further past the food court, we entered what looked just like a grocery store, but smaller.

"We keep track of everything that you get here," Joe said. "We obviously don't want to waste anything. But you'll notice in your quarters, there are no trash cans like there was in the program. There is a chute in your kitchen that sends all your 'waste' down to our recycling level. All the waste from the program ends up there as well." We walked through the grocery store, back to the elevator.

"Now the rest of the levels below this one are restricted until you've had your full psych evaluation," Joe said before hitting a button. "You'll get to see them today but won't be allowed in them again until you've been approved to do so. Understand?"

"Yes," I said, and Joe hit B16.

"B16 and 17 are our labs levels," Joe said. The elevator opened and it looked more like a greenhouse. "16 is mostly for food growth as well as artificial meat, since we can't very well have a farm underground." The plants were on shelves though, not in pots like a normal greenhouse. There were shelves and shelves of plants of all kinds. It definitely looked very efficient. Further down, there was a production line type thing that was spitting out what looked like ground beef.

"17 is our medical labs, as well as researching better ways to feed everyone," Joe continued. In the elevator again, we head to 18. The doors open to what has to be two floors opened up together. Huge machines were working all around the large area. There were sections cut off from the rest by chain link fences.

"This is our recycling level," Joe said, stepping off onto the catwalk above these machines. He didn't go far, just to the railing so we could look out over it all. "We recycle everything we use; leftover food and human waste gets turned into fertilizer for the new plants. Plastics, metals, and glass all gets recycled back into circulation. When we're cut off from our former natural resources, we have to make sure we don't waste anything." It was impressive that's for sure. He led me back into the elevator. He pressed B19.

"The last two levels are all dedicated to running the experiment," he explained. The doors opened to a computer control center. It looked advanced. There were screens on every inch of wall it seemed. There were at least 20 people in this very large room all busy with some screen here or some keyboard there. Most of them wore headsets and some were talking into them.

"Who are they talking to?" I asked pointing to a man talking into his headset.

"Some of them are talking to controllers in other areas, some of them are talking to controllers in the experiment itself. We have people planted inside that live there and who call in to report about anything and everything," Joe said calmly. "Your friend Ryan is one of our controllers." I whipped around to look at him.

"What?" I snap, probably a little too defensively. "Ryan knew about all this? She worked for you? She was lying to me?" I was angry, though I'm not entirely sure why, given that I was going to be doing the same thing.

"Yes," Joe replied. "She knew about all of this. She volunteered for it. She never had her memory blocked or anything. She has been with the program since the beginning about 10 years ago. Apparently, she had no problems with not sharing information with participates." His tone was so nonchalant, like what he was saying shouldn't affect me at all. But of course, it did. Obviously, I didn't actually know her as long as I thought I did, but it turns out I didn't know her hardly at all. I started wondering whether any of the stuff she told me was true. The only lie I have told her is that I'll be away on business for two weeks, she's been lying to me for 7 years.

I could see her on one of the far monitors, sitting at our bar, what was our bar, with John and Richard. I was prepared to fight this whole system just to make it so she didn't have to be together with that guy. For all I know, she wanted to be with him. I mean she's not required to follow the whole 'soulmate' thing considering she's in on it.

"Don't take it personally," Joe said calmly. "She was just doing her job." I opened my mouth to retort, to yell, but I closed it again.

"I'd like to go back to my quarters now," I said flatly. Joe nodded, still oblivious to my anger. We got back into the elevator, he hit B5.

"Oh," he exclaimed and pulled a bracelet from his pocket. "One more thing. We require everyone to wear one of these until they pass their psych eval. It's just a device to keep track of you if we need to." I held out my left hand and he put the bracelet around my wrist, it clicked into place, obviously designed by the same people who made the soulmate watches. I doubted I could get it off if I tried. Though it did tell the time, so that was new. The elevator doors opened, and I got out.

"Have a good night," Joe said as the doors shut. I went back to my quarters and opened my closet. I found a muscle shirt, shorts and tennis shoes. I changed and left my room again. I went to the elevator, I hadn't eaten all day, but I was too angry to eat. I hit B2, the recreational level.

I found the weight and exercise room. I had always been one to want to work out when I was pissed off. I grabbed a towel and a water from the corner, then found a treadmill and hopped on it. I was the only one in here this late, and there was music playing on the overhead speakers. I ran and ran and thought about everything. Allison, Ryan, this whole place, the War, my parents, my sister, everything. I ran for an hour before I got off the treadmill and found a bench press. I put 75 pounds on each side and laid down.

"Need a spotter?" I heard coming from the direction of the door. I nearly hit my head on the bar trying to sit up and look. Allison was walking towards me, in short shorts and a tank top. If I wasn't so angry still, I'd be struck with how gorgeous she looks.

"You scared me," I said dryly, not bothering to hide my mood, as I laid back down. "How'd you know I was here?"

"You always liked to work out if you were angry," she said standing above my head and looking down at me. "I figured Joe would have told you about Ryan by now and I knew you wouldn't take it very well." I raised my eyebrow at her.

"How long were you watching me after you got out?" I asked as I lifted the bar off the rack.

"As soon as I remembered enough," she said, "So a couple weeks after I got out. I even got assigned as Dr. Cooper's assistant on the inside so I could see you. Of course, I had a mask on, so you wouldn't have recognized me." I missed the rack trying to put it back quickly, she steadied it and I sat up, turning to face her.

"I do remember that!" I said. "You were new, and I thought you looked familiar. I kept checking out your ass too." She laughed and I couldn't help but crack a smile.

"Did you love her?" she asked suddenly, and I sighed heavily.

"Honestly," I said. "I think I could have, I think I would have fallen for her if it continued how it was the past week or so. And part of me did love her as a friend. But romantically, no."

"I thought I saw the signs," she said sheepishly. "I was concerned."

"Why's that?" I asked.

"How much do you remember yet?" she countered.

"I remember losing grip on your hand running to the fallout shelter," I said. "And I remember our first kiss under the bleachers. Though given what my letter from my past self said, I can infer a lot. My past self was convinced that you are the girl we're going to marry." She laughed and blushed.

"At one point, I think both our past selves would have said that," she said, brushing it off. "What else can you infer from your letter?"

"Given my threat to kill your foster dad, I'd say I was super protective of you," I said before thinking about it, and I saw a shadow cross her face. "Shit. I'm sorry. I told myself not to bring him up. I hadn't said what he did, but I could guess."

"That was one of the harder things for me to remember," she said dryly. "He's dead by the way. Neither of my foster parents made it to a shelter."

"Good," I said. "Hmm… I mentioned what happened that day and how tightly I held you while we wait it out. Again, infers to my protectiveness of you as well as how much I cared about you. And how I told them to take us together and how we had to be woken up together."

"I think you would have fought them if they had said no," she said laughing.

"Probably," I agreed. "I wrote about hugging you and kissing you and saying, 'I'll see you on the other side,' before they froze us. I remember saying that same thing before our first kiss under the bleachers."

"Under the bleachers, it was just to lighten the mood," Allison said, staring off as if remembering herself. "Before they froze us, it was to reassure me that it was okay. It was kind of our thing, you used to say it when we would get off the phone at night before…." She trailed off, that shadow on her face again. I stood up and took her hand, pulling her into my arms. I hugged her tightly and she hugged me back.

"I may not be able to remember exact moments yet," I said, speaking into the hair on top of her head. "But I remember the feeling when we kissed the first time and I remember feeling terrified when I lost the grip on your hand running to the shelter. I know that you mean a lot to me." I kissed the top of her head. "I may not know exactly why yet." We both laughed. "But I can live with that much for now. I have no intentions of going anywhere, you're stuck with me again." She laughed again, I could tell that she was crying. I hugged her for a while longer, until she pulled back. She turned wiping her eyes, trying to hide it from me.

"I don't know how I keep getting stuck with you," she said sarcastically. "You're like a lost puppy that keeps following me home." I pretended to be hurt, and she laughed.

"Hey at least I'm a cute puppy," I said as I laid back on the bench. "You could be stuck with Balding Joe." She laughed loudly.

"Oh my god!" she said. "That's a very fitting nickname. I'm gonna have to make sure I don't call him that when I'm talking to him." I laughed.

"I've had a hard time with it," I joked. "So, I gotta ask, were you jealous of how I was with Ryan in the program?"

"I cried," she said, "mostly happy tears, because the puppy would be following someone else home."

"Ouch. You cut me deep." She laughed and helped me put the bar back on the rack again. "I'm just going to imagine you were tear streaked, depressed and eating ice cream for at least a month."

"Please," she laughed. "You're barely worth cookie dough, let alone ice cream."

"You know, I don't remember you being so abusive to me," I lied.

"You must have me mixed up with your other girlfriends," she laughed.

We joked and laughed for another hour or so in the workout room, we didn't do much working out though. After that, it was past midnight and we headed to the elevator.

"So which floor are you on anyway?" I asked when we got into the elevator.

"I'm not telling," she said, shaking her head. "I don't trust you not to stalk me." I laughed.

"Oh, come on," I said holding up my new bracelet. "You literally get a tracker for me and I don't even get to know which floor you're on?" She laughed and hit the B5 button.

"Technically the government is tracking you, not me. Though that's a good idea. Maybe I can get clearance to your device…" she looked thoughtful.

"Oh no you don't," I said, and I grabbed her in a bear hug and—

I was in a bedroom, I'm assuming my bedroom. Allison was there and she was laughing, I had her in a bear hug. She was screaming for me to let go and I kissed her. She kissed me back, wrapping her arms around my neck. I walked her over to the bed and we laid down, still kissing.

--I pulled back and released her immediately. She looked surprised, but I was still in my memory.

"Are you okay, Leo?" she asked and then she put two and two together. "You just had a flashback, didn't you?" I nodded and the elevator door opened. She grabbed my hand and pulled me down the hall. "Come on."

I assumed we were going to my quarters, but she pulled me past number 513. We stopped further down at number 522. She put the palm of her free hand on the screen and the door clicked open. We walked into her quarters and she shut the door with her free hand. She pulled me in further, switching on the light as she went and pushed me to sit on the bed. I looked around. Her quarters looked exactly like mine in layout and furniture, but hers had a homier feel to them for some reason.

"Tell me what you saw," she said sitting in her desk chair.

"We were more than just good friends, weren't we?" I asked and she avoided my gaze.

"What did you remember?"

"Not much really," I said. "We were in, I'm assuming, my room and I had you in a bear hug just like I did in the elevator and you were screaming for me to let you go. And we were laughing, and I kissed you. You wrapped your arms around my neck, and I brought us over to the bed and we were still kissing. And then I was back in the elevator."

"Do you remember what I was wearing?" she asked.

"Why does that matter?" I asked, but she shot me a look and I closed my eyes to focus. "Um, it was a yellow shirt and jeans. Why?" She stood up and paced in front of me, like she wasn't sure if she wanted to tell me or how she would tell me. "Ally?" She stopped and looked at me.

"What did you say?" she asked, and I blinked. I closed my eyes again and I was in the crowd running toward the shelter again. I had her hand, but it was slipping.

"Ally," I said and opened my eyes. "That's what I yelled. I had remembered running to the shelter and losing grip on your hand, well my letter told me it was your hand, but I had remembered yelling something, but I couldn't remember what until just now. It was Ally, that's what I yelled. That's what I used to call you isn't it?" She sat in her chair again.

"Yes," She said, softly. "Or sometimes just Al, depending on what we were talking about. The reason I asked what I was wearing is because I had to be sure. Those two memories were on the same day. Our last day on the surface."

"But my letter said that you were over, and we were working on a project," I said, and she laughed.

"That was what we used to tell your parents," she said. "Hell, they treated me like family already, given... given my past. But they still wouldn't have been okay with us fooling around. We were young. I had come over and we were working on a project, until they left for the store. That memory of us kissing on the bed, was probably 10 minutes before the sirens went off."

We sat there looking at each other for a solid minute before she jumped up and took my hand, pulling me towards the door. "No more," she said. I stopped walking, and given the size difference, it stopped her easily.

"Why?" I asked.

"Because," she said. "Me telling you all this can affect how you remember your own memories. I could tell you that we were married and had three kids and eventually you would remember that we were married with three kids. It's just better if you remember it in your own time, that way you know it's real."

"I know you wouldn't lie to me," I said, still not leaving.

"Of course, I wouldn't," she said softly. "But trust me, it helps you process it all if you know it's real. Just, please trust me?" I smiled.

"I have a feeling I always have and always will," I said, being completely honest and she smiled.

"As will I," she said and kissed me on the cheek. "Now go to bed. We can hang out after I get off tomorrow, depending on what time you get done with Miss Anna. I get off at 6. Now go." She stamped her foot and opened the door. I smiled, leaned down and kissed her on the cheek.

"Night, Ally," I said as I walked out of her room and headed down the hall to mine.

I opened my door, walked in and leaned against the door after I closed it. I kicked off my shoes right by the door, peeled off my shirt and pulled off my shorts. I laid down in bed in just my underwear on top of the covers. I intertwined my fingers behind my head and sighed.

I knew that I cared about Ally. From how well we get along now and the few memories I can recall, that much was true. I didn't know how deep that feeling went, either now or then. My assumption was that it was a budding romance back then, that if things hadn't happened the way they did, we probably *would* be married with three kids by now. Well, not now now, but the appropriate amount of time back then. Unfortunately, right now, with my memory only coming in pieces, it can't be much more than a budding romance. It could grow to something more, for sure, when I get my memory back hopefully. But, without that history on both sides, it would be like starting from scratch, for me at least. I had a feeling that her feelings for me were just as deep now as they were then. I could grow to love her, even without the memories.

CHAPTER 7

"Can I tell you something?" a younger Ally asked me. She looked not much older than she would have been when we met.

"Of course," I say.

"You have to swear not to tell anyone," she said, and I nod, I could see tears welling up in her eyes. "My foster dad, Jim, he.... He comes into my room sometimes after everyone has gone to bed... and he touches me... like adults normally touch other adults..." The tears finally broke and she sniffled. "I don't like it... I tell him to stop and he just tells me to shut up, that he'll hurt me if I don't be quiet..." She was sobbing now. I pulled her toward me and held her until the shaking stopped.

"We have to tell someone Al," I said softly. "You know it's not right. He's not supposed to do that..." She shook her head hard.

"No," she said. "If we tell, then they'll move me to another foster family. The next one could be worse. This one is worse than the last one."

"Let me talk to my mom," I said insistently. "I promise she'll understand. Maybe she can help. She works with people that could help. Let me at least try, you shouldn't have to be going through that." She let out a shaky sigh.

"Okay," she said. "But I wanna stay in your room while you talk to her. I don't like talking about it." I nodded.

It was a different day, but about the same age. I was in the kitchen, talking to my mom and dad. My dad looked furious. He was tall, probably about 6'2, he had a beard and was very muscular.

"Mom," I said. "You should have seen her today. She was wearing long sleeves, but she showed me the bruises on her arms. We have to do something. She can't stay in that house anymore. He's molesting her and God knows what else is going on in there!"

"I already talked to child services," my mom said, tears in her eyes. "They said they're looking into it. Unfortunately, if she's not willing to talk about it, they will listen to her foster parents first. I know it's not a great system all the time sweetie."

"I'll go talk to him," my dad said, and mom shot him a look. "What? He'll live if that's what you're worried about."

"I don't know anything," my mom said and started wiping down the counter.

"Son, call Ally and tell her to come over," dad said, and I nodded. I did as I was told and Ally came over about 20 minutes later.

"I'll be back in a bit, love," dad said to mom and kissed her on the cheek. He ruffled Ally's hair as he walked by her. "Hi Ally, see you later."

"Are you hungry sweetie?" mom asked and made us some food.

Dad came back later that evening with a baseball bat over his shoulder and told Ally that she was staying over that night, that she could sleep in my bed and I would sleep on the couch. That night she snuck into the living room and snuggled up with me on the couch.

"I think my dad beat up your foster dad," I said quietly, and she giggled. "I'm being serious. He told my mom earlier that he would go talk to him and that 'he would live.' And then he comes back later with a baseball bat? Come on. You'll have to tell me what he looks like tomorrow."

"I would love your dad forever if he beat up Jim," she whispered.

"Apparently someone in my family will always protect you Al," I said and put my arm around her.

I'm older; probably high school age. Ally and I are walking through the hallway holding hands. A couple of football players are walking by us, laughing and looking at Ally. I'm confused and look at Allison, she's looking at her shoes avoiding looking at them.

"Hey Parks," one of them shouts from across the hall. I don't remember his name. "I'd be careful with that one, I hear she has a thing for older men." I whip around.

"What the fuck is that supposed to mean?" I snarl.

"I hear she was fucking her foster dad years ago and—" I'm across the hallway before he even has time to finish. I pin him to the lockers and start punching him in the face.

"Don't—ever—fucking—say—shit—like—that—again," I hit him with every word. His buddies are trying to pull me off of him.

"Leo Parks!" It's an older female teacher, I don't remember her name either. I release the jock and turn to face her. "What on earth are you doing? Go to the principal's office, now. You boys take him to the nurse."

Ally walks with me to the principal's office, obviously the teacher had called ahead, because he was standing outside his office waiting for me. Ally sat down outside the office and I went in, he closed the door.

"I've already called your father, he's on his way," he said as he sat behind his desk. I plopped down in the empty chair, still fuming. "Would you like to tell me why you were beating up Mr. Smith? Or would you rather wait until your father got here so you can explain it to him?"

"I'd rather wait," I said dryly, knowing my dad would take my side. So, we waited the 15 minutes for my dad to get there and I explained what happened. To my surprise, my dad agreed with the principal that I should be suspended, but he did fight to get the other boy a few detentions for his comments. The principal agreed.

"If you don't mind," my dad said, standing up. "I'd like to take Miss Sherrow home as well, I'm sure hearing that probably didn't have the best effect on her either." The principal nodded.

"I'll let the attendance office know," he said. We walked out of the office and Dad told Ally she was coming home with us.

"Do you know why I agreed with the principal son?" My dad asked when we were finally in the car. I shrugged, still angry. "Because even though you were defending Ally, and the other kid had no right to say those things, beating him up wasn't the way to go about it."

"You beat up Ally's foster dad," I snapped, and he laughed.

"You're right," he said. "I did. But I was willing to accept the punishment for doing so. He could have easily reported me to the police, and I could have been sent to jail for doing that. Even though we all know that he deserved it. I would have sat quietly in jail knowing that what I did was right. You have to realize that there are reactions to every action you take. Even a justified one. So, yes, what you did was justified, but you have to accept the punishment for it. Understand?"

"I guess," I mumble, still upset, but at least he admitted I was justified.

"And Ally," he said looking at her in the rearview mirror. "I'm sorry he said those things about you. He's just a stupid jock and probably couldn't get a beautiful girl like you to notice him. I'm glad Leo beat him up. Just don't tell his mother I said that." Ally laughed and I couldn't help but smile.

"Ally, are you still awake?" I asked and she rolled over to face me. High school age still. I know my parents know that we sneak together whenever she spends the night, because my dad had the sex talk with me. But apparently, they haven't wanted to do anything to stop it, probably because they know it makes Ally sleep better. She said she feels safer sleeping with me than alone.

"Yeah," she said, I reached over and touched her face softly.

"You know I love you right?" I said quietly, I could feel her smile beneath my hand, it was too dark to see anything definitive. I knew that she knew, but it was the first time I had said it out loud.

"I love you, Leo," she whispered, and I smiled as she leaned over and kissed me.

"There's been something I've wanted to give you," I said, reaching over in the dark to the drawer in my night stand, pulling out the chain with my class ring on it. I slid the chain over her head and could see her feeling it. "Consider it a promise ring."

"I love it," she said, I could hear the smile in her voice, and she pulled me in for another kiss.

* * *

I woke up to darkness and looked at my bracelet, 7:30. I groaned, I don't think I'm going to get used to this underground thing. Maybe there was a lamp in the store that I could set on a timer. I swung my feet over the edge of the bed, hating that my body was still on the sleep schedule I had in the experiment. I sat there for a minute staring into the darkness, thinking about all the memories I had remembered last night.

Now I knew what had happened with Ally's foster dad, and I know now that my dad beat his ass for what he had done. I was thankful for that. I would have liked to do that now knowing what he had done. And now I knew that I had loved Ally, through and through. I gave her my class ring, knowing that it would be taken as a promise for the future. I know that sounds cliché, but it means something to me to know that now.

I stood and walked to bathroom. Turning on the shower still thinking about everything. After my morning routine, I got dressed in some jeans and a t-shirt. I had noticed that they had taken my wardrobe from the experiment and brought it here for me. I hadn't noticed it last night since I was so angry after finding out about Ryan. I walked out my door and glanced down towards Ally's door, sure she was already at work by now. I headed to the elevator and hit B15. I wanted to wander the store for a bit and see what all they had.

The elevator doors opened and I realized that I was coming here right in the middle of the morning routine for some people. It was very crowded in the food court area. I stepped off the elevator as five people stepped on. I move out of the way and looked around at the options for food. I figured it was better to eat first, since I hadn't eaten since yesterday morning. I ended up with eggs, sausage, toast, and some coffee. I sat down at one of the empty tables and watched all the people busy moving about their morning.

By the time I was finished with my breakfast, the food court was nearly empty, as everyone was probably at their jobs by now. I stood and emptied my tray in one of the chutes labeled 'waste' and headed to the store on the other end of the floor. I grabbed one of the small baskets by the front door and wandered through the store. It was bigger than I had thought when we walked through yesterday. There was a grocery section, a small clothing section, cleaning supplies, a very small decorative section, and a practicality section. It was in that last section that I found a small desk lamp that I could set on a timer. Apparently, I wasn't the only one with the thought of having an artificial sun in their room. I picked up some groceries and even got a small picture to hang on my wall. It was a picture of a beautiful lake, you could see the green grass in the foreground and snow-topped mountains in the back.

After I put my groceries in my kitchen and hung my small picture opposite my bed, I changed and headed to the recreational level again. There obviously wasn't a lot to do here, so I might as well stay in shape. I ran on the treadmill for an hour or so and then lifted weights for another hour or two. Afterwards, I went back to my quarters to shower and have a sandwich for lunch.

I sat in my computer chair as I ate my sandwich and searched some history on my computer. I learned that War World III was predicted as early as 2017. Most people believed it was inevitable at that point. Tensions were too high across the world and they built up until they finally broke and caused basically a world ending event. An event scientists called a 'nuclear winter,' that made the surface uninhabitable. They are unsure when it will become habitable again but are still running tests to see if it will be.

Still running tests? I wonder why Balding Joe didn't mention that, maybe it's not pertinent information or this was written years ago, and they have given up hope. I'll have to ask when I see him again. I read through more of it. It mentions the possibility of it becoming habitable years later, but that was only theoretical. I'm curious how many years it will take, I personally would love to see the sun again, the real sun. I shake my head and decide to take a nap before Miss Anna comes over. I lay down on the bed with thoughts of the sun in my mind.

* * *

I blow out my candles. My 5th birthday party again. I look over at my mother who snaps a picture of me with my cake. I look around the room, there are a lot of boys my age around the table, all wearing party hats. Their mothers, I'm assuming that's who all these women are, are around the room. Talking and laughing amongst themselves. My dad is standing in the corner holding a younger girl in his arms. I know it's my little sister, Amanda, she is wearing an oxygen line on her nose and she doesn't have any hair.

"Happy birff-day, Leo," she said clapping her hands and grinning.

"Thanks, Manda-panda," I say as I stand up and hug her in my dad's arms. Dad ruffles my hair.

"Happy birthday little man," he said. "I'm gonna go start the burgers, Carol." He kisses my mom and hands Amanda to her.

"Who wants to play in the backyard?" she yells and all the boys cheer and run to the back door. I stop and hug my mom.

"I love you mom," I said. "Thanks for the party." She hugs me back and then pats my butt as I follow my friends.

"Go have fun sweetie," I hear her say before the door closes. I feel the sun on my face as I jump off the deck and into the grass of our backyard. I love the feeling of the sun, especially when there is a cool breeze outside. I look over and see my dad and the other dads all standing around the grill. I wave to him and he waves back.

* * *

I'm awoken by a knock on my door, I stand up and go to open the door. Miss Anna walks in with her briefcase and a different pants suit today.

"Hi Miss Anna," I say as I pull a chair from my table and bring it closer to hers at my desk.

"Hello Leo," she says, digging in her briefcase for her pen and paper again. She clicks it and looks at me. "So, what new memories have we remembered since yesterday."

I sit back in my chair and try to recall everything in my head in the past 24 hours. "I remember more about me and Ally."

"Oh?" she asked, pen poised over her pad.

"Actually," I say. "A lot more. I remembered when she told me about what her foster dad did to her. I remember my dad beating him up for it. I remember when I beat up a kid in high school for saying inappropriate things to her. I got suspended for that, which my father backed completely. I remember giving her my class ring and telling her to consider it a promise ring. I know that I loved her. I remembered kissing her before the sirens went off. She said it was like 10 minutes before the sirens."

"You've spoken to her about all this?"

"No, just that last one. The others were last night while I was sleeping. And just now, before you came, I remember more of my 5th birthday party. My little sister was there."

"Amanda, right?" she asked glancing over at my file that was still scattered all over my desk.

"Yes, I called her Manda-Panda at my party. She was already sick then. She died about a year later."

"And how do you feel about that?"

"I'm not really sure," I said honestly. "Of course, it's sad. She was so young. I know I loved her and that I always will. But I didn't get to know her that well. I was 6 when she died. I didn't know much of anything then." She continued to scratch away on her notepad. "I remember the sun. I mean, of course I would, but like my birthday party? I remember going outside to play with my friends and feeling the sun on my face and a cool breeze. I miss that. Are we ever going to be back on the surface? I was reading that even after nuclear war, it takes time for the planet to recover, but it can."

"Oh honey," she said with a soft smile. "I'm definitely not the person to be asking that. I'm just a simple counselor and certainly not a scientist. I hope it'll happen in my lifetime, but we'll see. Now, are you planning about talking to Allison about all this?"

"Definitely," I said without hesitation. "I knew we had a connection when we met yesterday, I knew there was something there. I felt like I had known her for years and I have. Of course, I don't remember everything yet, but I know that she means the world to me. Even now."

"And how do you feel about Ryan now?" she asked, and I was kind of shocked by the question. Though I shouldn't have been. Of course, she knew about everything in the experiment.

"Honestly," I said slowly. "I agreed to this whole thing, the being pulled out, to try and get Ryan out of it as well. Or at least to get her out of that relationship. But now that I know that she's known from the beginning, that she's been lying to me for years? I'm not sure how I feel. I know part of me still cares about her but I can't help that. Those feelings were real. At least for me. I'm not sure if she feels the same. I would love to ask her, to ask her if any of it was real."

"Were you in love with her?" she asked, and I laughed.

"Ally asked me the same thing last night," I said. "I told her the truth. I think I could have fallen for her if it had continued, but now that I know all of it was a lie? No, not romantically, no. Like I said, I'll always care for her, but I can't trust her now. Ally hasn't lied to me. Hell, she's even avoided telling me the truth to make sure I remember it for myself. She doesn't want to influence my memories by telling me how she felt or feels. I can tell she cares for me. I'm not sure if Ryan ever truly cared for me. Trust is a big thing for me and she broke that."

"Why is trust a big thing for you?"

"I'm honestly not sure," I say trying to remember more. "I know that with each new memory that is coming back, I feel trust for the people in them. My mother, my father, Allison. The emotions are stronger than the memories themselves sometimes. The love, the trust, the loyalty. Now when I think back to memories of Ryan, I feel anger and confusion. I'm not sure what to feel for her now. I wanna talk to her, but I'm not sure I'll have the chance until I'm cleared to go back into the experiment."

"Hmm," she said. "I might be able to arrange something, to help you sort through all of this of course. I can't guarantee anything, but I'll try."

"I would appreciate that," I said. "Anything would help at this point. I'm totally lost when it comes to her."

"And Allison?"

"I know I care about her, I know I loved her before, I know that I could grow to love her again. With or without the memories. I can't describe it, we have a connection, the more time I spend with her, the more that connection strengthens. I don't know if it's because of how much we were together when we were younger, or its just what was meant to be, as cliché as that sounds." I laugh at myself. "But I like it, I like how at home I feel around her, even yesterday, before I knew anything. I felt at home."

"And you want to continue to strengthen that connection? No matter what, I assume?"

"For sure," I said. "I don't know of anything that would make me not want to."

"Interesting," she said and scratched away.

"Why is it interesting?" I asked.

"You're the first patient I've had that has so quickly decided to basically let go of everything that happened in the experiment," she said, and I cocked my head to the side.

"Is that a bad thing?"

"No, just interesting. Most of the others take longer to separate themselves from what happened inside, some of them never completely separate themselves."

"I mean, yes it happened," I said. "I'm not denying it. If I had my memory while I was in there I would have spent the whole time trying to find Ally. She would have been my soulmate if any of it was real, but it was rigged. It was all rigged. So why would I let some rigged program dictate my life? It was physically real, yes, but mentally? Emotionally? None of it was real as far as I'm concerned."

"Does that mean the feelings you have for Ryan, the caring for her, isn't real?"

I opened my mouth to respond but closed it. I had not thought about it like that. "I mean, no. But if it wasn't rigged, I wouldn't have felt those things for her. They probably put Ally and I in opposite ends of the experiment to make sure we wouldn't find each other accidently. That's not fair." I was on my feet by this point, pacing behind my chair. "It doesn't make any sense, it makes me angry. The life that Ally and I could have had by now had they not picked us for some stupid experiment. We could have had kids by now. How does that help a fertility experiment to not let people who were already together be together in the experiment? Why bother?"

"Are you angry at the people for putting you in there? Or are you angry at yourself for not remembering her while you were in there?" she asked, I stopped pacing, staring at the wall.

"Both," I said quietly after a minute. "I loved her so much, I can feel that. Surely something like that, an emotion that strong, would have won out. I would have remembered her, I should have. I could have saved her from all that shit, God knows who they put her with. I protected her for so long, just to fail so badly."

"You had an implant in your brain that blocked those memories, those feelings. You can't blame yourself for that. She didn't remember you in there either. She isn't going to blame you and you shouldn't either. You are not all powerful, Leo. You can't protect her from everything. How is she ever going to learn to be independent if you fight all her battles for her?"

"If I'm always around, why would she need to be independent?" I countered jokingly. I resumed my pacing. "I know, I know. That's not the point and it's wrong to even imply that I don't want her to be independent."

"Maybe that's why they didn't put you two together in there," she said lightly. "Maybe they wanted to see how you both would do independently of each other. You guys were practically inseparable from what I've read in both of your files, maybe they thought you would evolve better separately for a while." I again stopped pacing and looked at her, thinking. She had a point.

"That would make sense," I said slowly. "Though I didn't evolve much."

"I disagree," she said. "You used to handle issues with violence, yet when you confronted with Richard you could have reacted the same way, but you didn't. You were the bigger person and sat there quietly, being respectful of Ryan. That shows some evolution."

"I really wanted to punch him," I smirked, sitting down again. "I guess you have a point. I wonder how Ally did in there."

"You should ask her," she smiled. "I think you'll be surprised." I cocked my head to the side again, she obviously knew something I didn't. Though that's not saying much nowadays. She looked at her watch. "I think we'll call it a day, after all, Ally got off work about 30 minutes ago." She picked up everything that belonged in my folder and put it neatly back in. She put that and her pen and pad back into her briefcase and stood to leave. "Tell her I said hello, will you?"

"Yes ma'am," I said and smiled, walking over to open the door.

"Same time tomorrow, Leo," she said as she was leaving.

"Yes ma'am," I said again and entered the hallway myself, closing the door behind me.

CHAPTER 8

I walked the opposite direction from Miss Anna, heading towards Ally's quarters. I knocked on the door and saw Miss Anna getting in the elevator at the end of the hall. Ally's door swung open, she was still wearing her scrubs from work. "Hi there," she said smiling, she stepped aside so I could come in. I did so and sat on her bed. "I just walked in like 5 minutes ago, was a little late getting off today."

"I hate it when that happens," I say with a smirk and she shoots me a sarcastic look.

"Very funny," she said. "I'm going to change but tell me how your day was." She was rummaging away in her closet.

"It was pretty boring to be honest. Went down and had breakfast and went to the store. I can't stand waking up to darkness," I said, laying back on her bed. She laughed.

"That's how I felt. I got one of those lamps too," she said nodding to her desk, on which sat a lamp just like the one I had gotten today. She grabbed up her clothes that she picked out and headed to the bathroom, leaving the door partially open. "Trust me, it's way better than the darkness or those crappy fluorescent lights early in the morning."

"Good," I said. "Because that was terrible this morning. Hmm. After that I went and worked out, then came back and took a shower and poked around on the computer for a bit. Then Miss Anna came by. She said hi, by the way."

"How did that go?" she asked loud enough for me to hear from the bathroom.

"Good," I said nonchalantly. She poked her head out the door, I could tell she didn't have a shirt on by her bare shoulders.

"You're a terrible liar, you know that right?" she said, and I laughed as she pulled her head back in the bathroom.

"Okay, okay," I said. "You were our topic of conversation and how I felt about not remembering you while I was in the experiment." She came out of the bathroom and sat in her desk chair close to the bed facing me. I rolled on my side, my head propped on my hand so I could look at her.

"How do you mean?" she asked.

"I used to protect you," I said. "I had a few memories come back to me last night after we talked. I remembered when you told me what Jim did to you. I remember the night my dad went and beat his ass for it. I remember beating up that guy in high school for what he said about you. And I remember giving you my class ring." She pulled the chain around her neck out of her shirt. There was my class ring.

"This class ring?" she asked, jokingly putting on her finger, it was way too big.

"Yes, that class ring," I said. "'Consider it a promise ring,' that's what I said when I gave it to you… I felt like I was your protector. Your knight in shining armor, as stupid as that sounds. So, in there, I didn't remember you, I feel bad about that. I didn't save you."

"I didn't remember you either," she said, putting her legs over mine. "You can't blame yourself for that, that's dumb. You had a brain implant, just like the rest of us."

"That's what Miss Anna said," I replied. "She also said that maybe they put us in there separately to help us evolve some. And then she told me to ask you how your time in there was." She laughed.

"Her and I had a similar conversation when I came out," she said lightly. "I didn't understand why they would put us in there separately when we were already together if it was truly about fertility. We could have had like seven kids by now." I hold up my hands.

"Hey now," I said jokingly. "Who said we're having seven kids?"

"I did," she said matter-of-factly.

"Okay, fair enough," I nodded, and she laughed.

"But to answer your question," she continued. "I did evolve while I was in there. Before I went in there, I was this terrified young girl who could hardly look at men, because of what happened. Granted, I still don't like to talk about it, it's definitely not one of my favorite memories. But I got to go in there with a clean slate so to speak. I learned martial arts, I learned how to be confident and I wasn't afraid anymore. I'm still not, it helped me through it all, even after I got my memories back. So as much as I love that you defended me, and that you still want to save me, I don't need saving anymore. I'm not a damsel in distress. I can handle myself now."

"Well, shit," I said, sitting up and pretending to stand up. "You obviously don't need me anymore." Her foot came up to my chest and pushed me back on the bed. She crawled out of her chair, onto the bed and straddled me. Her hands were on my chest holding me down and her knees were on either side of my hips.

"Just because I said I don't need saving, doesn't mean I don't need you," she said, and I smiled.

"I'm not complaining." She laughed and leaned down to kiss me. It was electrifying. She pulled back and rested her forearms on my chest looking at me.

"I think we both grew in our own ways," she said thoughtfully. "But I don't want to be the girl you push behind you to protect. I wanna be fighting beside you." I reached up and brushed the strand of hair in her face behind her ear.

"I'm definitely okay with that," I said softly. "You've got to give me a bit to get used to it. Habits are hard to break." She laughed.

"That's fair," she said.

"Now…" I grab the inside of her arm and hook my leg behind hers, flipping her over in one fail swoop. "I'm curious to see what you got." I grinned and she laughed.

"I don't think you could handle it, Parks," she said, and I laughed.

"Try me, Sherrow."

"You asked for it." I have no idea how to describe what she did, I'm not even sure I understand how she did what she did next. It was like one minute she was under me, my knees between her thighs, my hands on the bed under her arms. Then the next minute she was monkey crawling over my body and then I was on my back in an arm bar between her legs. I tap my hand on her leg to get her to let go of me.

"Well, shit," I said. "I was not expecting that at all." She laughed.

"I told you, you couldn't handle it."

"You were not lying," I said as I rubbed my shoulder. "You're gonna have to teach me some of that."

"Maybe." She straddled me again. "Maybe I like being in charge sometimes." She kissed me again.

"I won't complain about that," I said leaning up to kiss her again, she pulled back from me and pushed my chest back down to the bed.

"Are you hungry?" she asked grinning. "I'm starving." I groaned as she got off me and the bed.

"Okay, that, I will complain about," I said, and she laughed. I mock pouted as I sat up. "You're just gonna leave me hanging like that?" She matched my pouting face and came to stand between my knees. She gave me one quick kiss, before going to sit in her desk chair to put her shoes on.

"You're such a guy. You'll be fine, you big baby," she said, and I laughed. "I really am hungry though. I didn't get a chance to eat lunch. You buying?"

"For you my lady, always," I said. I stood up and bowed.

"Such a gentleman," she said with a smirk as she stood too. "Maybe I can keep you around as my man servant."

"Oh, that's how it's gonna be huh?" I say walking towards her. "I'd rather be a caveman." I reached down and picked her up over my shoulder, swatting her ass as I carried her towards the door.

"Put me down, Leo!" she yelled and slapped my back, laughing.

"Me. Man. Find girl," I say, grunting. She poked me in the side and I am apparently ticklish. I jumped a little and shifted her so she was in both my arms in front of me. "No fair! I didn't know I was ticklish there." She laughed and I leaned down to kiss her.

"All's fair in love and war, baby," she said laughing as I put her feet down. She pulled me down by my neck for another kiss. "Come on. You're making me hungrier."

"I had another feeling in mind," I say slyly. She hit my chest and laughed. She grabbed my hand and pulled me towards the door.

We head down to the food court and settle on Chinese food for dinner. We got our food and went to find an empty table to sit at. Apparently it was prime dinner time. There weren't a lot of empty tables. We found one near the back corner by the store and sit opposite each other. We sat there eating, talking, laughing, and sharing off each other's plates. It felt like old times, well, what I could remember of old times.

"So how do you still have my class ring?" I asked. "I'm surprised they didn't take it from you in the experiment."

"They did," she said, still eating. "Or they wanted to. But I convinced them to let me put it in the envelope with my letter to myself. Since it wasn't very big, they said that was fine. I had to explain to myself what it was since I didn't remember yet. I've had it on ever since. Why? You want it back?" I laughed.

"Not a chance," I said. "I meant what I said when I gave it to you. And I told you, you're stuck with me again." She laughed. "Hell, it probably doesn't even fit anymore." She took the chain off from around her neck and pulled my hand towards her. She tried to put it on my finger, but it barely got past the first joint. We both laughed.

"I was skinny back then," I said, as she put it back around her neck. "I saw the picture they had of me in my file. I was a twig."

"You were definitely tall and lanky," she agreed and laughed.

"I don't know what you saw in me," I said in mock sarcasm.

"I'm still trying to figure it out," she said with a smirk.

"So savage," I joke. "I'm not sure I can be in such an abusive relationship."

"Who said we were in a relationship?" she countered, and I laughed.

"Okay, that's fair," I say putting my hands up and leaning back. "How many guys do you got lined up that I gotta fight? Maybe your 'soulmate' from the program?" I laughed, but something crossed her face that stopped me. "What's wrong?"

"I'm assuming they did it to test me," she started slowly. "To see how far I had come. But the 'soulmate' they paired me with was an asshole. He was nice the first week or so, but then he got mean. He hit me and cut me off from my friends. He wanted me all to himself he would say, and that he wanted dinner on the table when he got home. The first time he hit me, I was so shocked that I didn't react. He apologized and I accepted it. I mean he was my soulmate, right? Surely, I wasn't meant to be in an abusive relationship for forever. It was just a mistake. But it happened again and after the third time I was ready for him. I had a bat with me and I used it. I beat him until he stopped moving and then I ran. That was the night they pulled me out of it."

"What did they say?" I asked, angry again at this whole place.

"They told me about the experiment and how it was all rigged," she was staring at her hands. I reached over and took them with mine. She smiled, took a breath and continued. "They told me that he, my soulmate, was a plant, like Ryan was. That he was there to see how far I had evolved. They had expected me to just leave him, not to defend myself. They said they couldn't blame me. They told me he had lived, but that he had a long recovery ahead of him. I didn't care. I still don't. I'm not sorry. If you take a job where you have to abuse a woman, or anyone for that matter, to see how they'll react, then you deserve the consequences of it. There's a reaction to every action you take." I smiled and squeezed her hand.

"My dad said that," I said.

"I know," she replied. "That's where I got it from. It's stuck with me for years. But anyway, they have him down on the recycling level now. Apparently, the damage I did to him made it hard for him to think very well. So they keep him down there doing basic stuff. I've seen him a couple times here or in the elevator. He kind of puts his head down and avoids me and I just ignore him. I won't be a victim again. Fuck that."

"You really have evolved," I say squeezing her hand again. "I'm so proud of you. I was ready to go find him and beat his ass, but you've obviously did that just fine." She laughs. "It's gonna take some getting used to, you fighting your own battles, but I think I can live with that. You are an amazingly strong and confident woman now. I've never been prouder of anyone in my life. Well at least that I remember." She laughed again.

"That means a lot," she said and smiled. "We can take on whatever the world throws at us now."

"Well," I said looking around. "Given how small our world is now, I think it's just gonna be mostly drama." She laughed.

"You aren't kidding," she said, taking one of her hands back to continue eating. "I wonder if the surface will ever be livable again. I'm getting tired of this already."

"I was just talking to Miss Anna about that earlier," I say. "I asked when it would be livable again, but she said she didn't know. That she's no scientist. I was looking it up on the computer before and it said that even after a nuclear war the planet can recover. It just takes a while. It's been what? 70 something years? How long does it take?"

"That's what I've been wondering too," she said quietly leaning forward. "But I highly doubt we are supposed to be talking about it."

"Why?"

"I brought it up to someone I worked with months ago and he shushed me and walked away," she whispered. "So, later."

No sooner had I nodded, Balding Joe walked up to our table. I leaned back in my chair.

"Hi Joe," I say, still borderline sarcastic with him.

"Hello Leo," he said as he nodded to me and then Ally. "Allison. Leo, I wanted to check in on you. See how you're doing?"

"I'm fine," I say. I don't know what it is, but I don't think I'll ever really like him. "Settling in just fine. Thanks for the concern."

"Good, good," he said. "Glad to hear it. Well, I'll leave you two to your dinner. Have a good night." He walked away and I raised an eyebrow at Ally. She shook her head.

"Damn Balding Joe," I mutter with a grin and she laughs.

"Stop that," she whispers.

"I've been wanting to hit up the library, you in?" I ask, pushing my empty plate away from me.

"Sure," she said, standing and grabbing her tray. We dumped our waste and headed back to the elevator. "I'll show you my favorite spot."

We got off on the library floor and Ally took my hand, dragging me to the right. We went past shelves and shelves of books and she kept turning corners. I would never find my way out on my own. Finally, we ended up in this almost secluded corner of the library. It was impossible to see the main desk in the middle from here. There was a couch against the wall.

"Looks cozy," I said, looking around. "You're gonna have to lead me back out of here later, because I'm never finding my way out alone." She laughed.

"This is the fiction section," she said. "Mostly romance and mystery, sci-fi is a little further down. Non-fiction is the other side of the floor."

"If I'm not back in an hour send out a search party," I joke and kiss her before wandering down some aisle at random, reading titles as I go.

Eventually I find a book that seems interesting and I find my way back to our couch in the corner. I sit there and start reading, Ally comes back shortly after with a book of her own. She lays with her head on the arm rest and her legs across my lap. I rest my hands on her legs and we stay like that reading. Occasionally making the other read a funny part in our book. It was nice, super comfortable, and easy to just be sitting there reading with her.

After a few hours, I checked my watch and it was almost midnight. I poked Ally's leg on my lap and looked over at her. I realized that she was asleep, I decided not to wake her. I moved her legs off me so I could stand up. I picked her up easily and headed towards the elevator. It took me a minute to find my way, but once I did, I hit B5.

Getting her hand on her door was more difficult without dropping her or waking her, but eventually I managed, and her door popped open. I carried her in and kicked the door shut behind me. I laid her gently on the bed and pulled off her shoes. I covered her with her blanket. Brushing the hair out of her face I kissed her forehead. She squirmed a bit but slept on. I turned off the light and left quietly, heading to my own door. After undressing I passed out easily on my bed.

* * *

I'm standing in a field. Looking around I see that the trees that were once standing around this area have all been pushed over and look charred. The ground itself is green and I see smaller, younger trees all around growing up through the burned ones. I start walking in the opposite direction that the trees are laying. I can see flowers growing here and there, still small, like they haven't been growing for long. I keep walking until I'm on the edge of a giant crater. A part of me knows this is where one of the bombs hit. But even here I can see green grass pushing up through the dirt in the crater. Very sparse compared to the rest of the area, but it was there.

The surface was livable again. I heard a noise and turned around, there was a young deer, a fawn, walking through the area I just passed through. It stopped and looked at me for a minute as if unsure what to think of me, then it kept walking. I smiled. I wasn't sure if any of the animals would survive the war but obviously they had. At least some of them. I looked up over the crater and I could see buildings in the distance. I decided it would better to walk around the crater. Just in case there was some leftover radiation.

Eventually I reached the buildings, or what was left of them. There were people here, living in these buildings, surviving is more accurate. They looked bruised and malnourished, but they were alive. I wanted to talk to them. To ask them how long they had been there. How long the surface was like this, but they all seemed scared of me. I looked down and realized that I was holding a gun and I was wearing a military uniform. There were others behind me all dressed the same and a large truck behind them. We were marching through the city and the people seemed terrified of us. I wonder what had happened to them. What had been done to them. As we were walking a man tried to run across the road in front of us but tripped. I raised my rifle and shot him face down in the road.

* * *

CHAPTER 9

I woke with a start, covered in sweat. I sat up and rubbed my eyes trying to sort out the dream I just had. It had to have been a dream and not a memory. There's no way I would shoot someone laying in the dirt already. Let alone shoot anyone. I may not have known who I was, but I know who I am. That's just not something I would do. I know it. I looked at my bracelet to see the time, 3:35am.

I groaned and got up to use the bathroom. I stood at the sink and splashed water on my face then stared at myself in the mirror. It was a bad dream. Not a memory. That's all it was, don't over think it. It was just a bad dream. That's not who you are.

I head back to my bed and just as I'm about to get back in it, there's a knock on my door. Who could that be? I go over and open the door, Ally is standing there wrapped in her blanket.

"What's wrong, Al?" I step out of the way so she can come in. "Are you okay?"

"I had a bad dream," she said softly. "And I'm off tomorrow—or today, whatever. So, I thought we could cuddle?"

"I had a bad dream too," I say shutting the door and walking back over to my bed. "At least I hope it was a dream." We both crawl into my bed and get under the covers, we're facing each other, and she automatically winds her legs around mine. She's warm.

"What was your dream about?" she asked. I explained it to her.

"I'm assuming it was a dream," I said. "Because I haven't remembered anything else about being in the military. And it was obviously after the war and I was frozen and then I was with you here. Was I ever in the military?"

"No," she said. "Not that I know of at least. After we went in the experiment, who knows what happened though. They messed with our memories before. But you wouldn't kill anyone, not like that at least. That's not who you are."

"I know," I say. "I'm sure it was just a dream. What was yours about?"

"Jim and Carl," she said coldly.

"Carl was your soulmate in the program I'm assuming?"

"Yes." I wrap my arms around her and pull her close.

"It's over now," I say. "You always slept better with me. That's why my parents never said anything about us sneaking together." She pulled back so she could look at me.

"Wait, they knew?"

"You didn't know?" I asked, glad to know something she didn't for once. She shook her head and I laughed. "They never told me straight out that they knew, but my dad gave me the sex talk earlier than he would have I'm betting." She laughed.

"Not that it was needed, with us anyway," she said, I cocked my head to the side, and she did the same. "Wait. You thought—you thought that we had… that we had had sex?" I felt myself blush and I was hoping that it was dark enough that she couldn't see it.

"I mean," I started. "I hadn't remembered it, no, but I just assumed… you had said that we fooled around…" She laughed.

"No," she said still laughing, she pulled away from me, rolling onto her back. "No, I mean, we've done some other things, but we never had sex."

"Well, now I feel stupid," I said bitterly, I rolled onto my back and she stopped laughing. She rolled onto her side again, her head resting on one of her hand, the other on my chest.

"Hey," she said softly. "I didn't mean to make you feel that way. It wasn't because we didn't want to. It was because I was not as... stable as I would have liked back then. After everything with Jim... as much as I trusted you, there was just a line I couldn't cross back then. We came close a few times, but I would always end up breaking down, ruining the moment. Though you would never tell me that I ruined the moment, you would always just hold me and reassure me. And now that we're back it's not like we're exactly running like we used to, given your memory situation." I sigh.

"I guess that makes sense," I said. "I just feel stupid for assuming it. It's not like I haven't had sex before, you know?" She giggled.

"I'm sure the ladies were lining up to get a piece of that action," she said, and I laughed. "It'll happen when it's the right time." I sighed overdramatically and she laughed again.

"I guess I'll wait," I said sarcastically. "Though you're right there's girls lining up for this action, so you might miss out."

"I'm sure I can take any one of them," she replied in stride. "I have dibs."

"Do you now?" I asked, feigning shock. "Does that mean I can call dibs too?"

"Definitely," she said, pulling me in for a kiss. I took the kiss deeper, twisting my tongue around hers, she tasted amazing. She pulled me harder and closer to her, digging her fingers into my neck. I feel her nails in my back and I moan, pulling back.

"Be careful, the right time could be sooner than you think," I said, and she giggled.

"I haven't tasted you in so long," she said seductively. "It's like a drug." She kissed me again, taking control of it and biting my bottom lip, I moaned again. She pushed me on my back and straddled me. She grabbed my chin and pushed my face to the side, kissing along my jawline slowly. I groan as she reaches my ear, I can feel her breath on my ear and neck. She bites my ear and I moan louder.

"You're enjoying torturing me, aren't you?" I ask as I squeeze her hips. She giggles and takes both my hands off her hips and pins them above my head. She slides her tongue from my ear down to my neck and bites hard. I suck in my breath as I try to control my urge to flip her over and rip her clothes off. "You're making this extremely difficult, you know that right?"

"Yes," she whispered in my ear, running her tongue along the outside. "I'm making it difficult for myself too." I laughed as I leaned up and bit her neck while she was busy with my ear. She moaned and it was the most provocative sound I had ever heard. She pulled back, her hands still holding mine above my head. "That wasn't fair."

"All's fair in love and war baby," I said repeating what she had told me earlier and I laughed. "It's not fair that I'd be the only one all hot and bothered."

"Ok, that's fair," she said nodding. She released my hands but didn't get off of me. She raised her eyebrow and grinned. "You weren't lying about being hot and bothered, were you?" I blushed again, knowing that she could feel my hardness beneath her.

"I don't remember you being such a brat," I said, running my hands up her thighs and squeezing as I neared the top. Her head tilt back, and her eyes closed.

"You love my being a brat," she said, and she leaned down to kiss me softly. She got off me and laid beside me again. I breathed deeply, trying to regain control of my blood flow. "You going to make it babe?"

"You started this," I said dryly, and she laughed.

"That's fair," she said. "I don't deny it."

"Just give me a minute," I said, and she laughed again. "You better quit laughing or I'm gonna bite you again." Her laughter turned into quiet giggling and I sighed. "You're gonna be the death of me."

"You're not allowed to die," she said. "Not when I finally got you back again."

"Yes, ma'am," I say sarcastically, she hit my chest.

"I'm being serious," she said pouting. "That would just be mean." I put my arm around her, wrapping my legs in hers like earlier.

"I have no intention of going anywhere, Al," I said softly, kissing her forehead. "I'm yours, through and through."

"Mmmm," she said as she snuggled closer to me, I wrapped her up tighter in my arms and pulled the blanket over us. She fell asleep quickly, though I don't know how. I was still worked up, so it took me a bit to fall asleep.

* * *

I woke up alone, though I wasn't in my quarters anymore. I was in a barracks sort of thing. There were bunkbeds all lined up throughout the room. I was on the top bunk, I heard sirens outside. My first thought was another bombing, but I didn't think so. I got up and put my pants and boots on quickly, running outside with everyone else. There were people trying to climb the fence that surrounded our area. I followed the rest of the people to the armory. I grabbed a rifle and a few magazines and went back outside, taking my position close to the fence. I opened fire on the people climbing the fence. Cutting them down like trees, they fell off the fence easily.

They looked bruised and malnourished, just like the people I had seen in the city before. They didn't appear to have any weapons on them, maybe they thought sear numbers would win out. A few of them made it completely over the fence before they were cut down as well. There was so much blood, I was covered in it by the time the assault stopped.

"Cease fire!" I heard behind me, though most of us had already. I looked around at the others, we didn't appear to have any injured on our side, but it was hard to tell with all the blood. We were ordered to go outside the fence and get these bodies away from it. I went out with a few others, rifles over our shoulders just in case. When we got close to the pile of bodies, I realized that a couple were still alive. They were coughing, spitting up blood. They weren't going to last long, that much I knew. I rolled one of the ones off the top of the pile and I thought I recognized someone further underneath. I pushed a few more bodies out of the way and looked again.

"Leo…" my father said in a raspy breath as blood poured from his mouth.

* * *

I sat bolt upright and jumped out of bed, heading for the toilet. I threw up just as I reached it. I was covered in sweat again, I continued to empty my stomach until I was just dry heaving.

"Leo?" I heard behind me, I knew it was Ally. She came over and rubbed my back. I was still dry heaving and couldn't get any words out. She stood and got a wash cloth, she wet it in the sink and put it on my neck.

I finally was able to catch my breath some in between hurls. I shut the door and I turned on the shower, I didn't want to be heard. Ally gave me a look and I held up a finger. It was still hard to talk at the moment.

"What's going on?" she asked, using the wash cloth to wipe my face when I finally sat on the floor with my back against the tub. She flushed the toilet and sat beside me.

"I had another dream," I said slowly. "I'm starting to think it wasn't a dream or that other one." I told her what happened, about seeing my father dead by my hand probably.

"But how is that possible?" she asked. "They told us your parents didn't make it to a shelter. And this is still counting on the fact that you served in the military after the war. The only time that would make sense is after we were put in the program, but that would be a lot of memory tampering. It's not safe to do it a lot."

"What if the surface is habitable?" I asked. "What if they're keeping us down here because they don't want us to know? Why else would that guy shush you when you asked about it? Something is going on. It doesn't make sense for me to be having dreams about the military and the surface if it didn't happen."

"I agree it's weird, Leo," she said softly. "But they could just be that, dreams. Your mind is still trying to sort through all the memories that are coming back. You seeing your dad dead by your hand could just be survivors' guilt. It doesn't mean it's real." She touched my face softly.

"But what about the other one?" I counter. "Killing some random guy in the middle of the street?"

"I don't know," she said. "But like I said your brain is going through a lot. I agree it's weird, and I agree it's odd that they don't want us to talk about the surface, but I don't want you to do anything crazy like running up there all because of these dreams. Okay? We can try to investigate it more if you want to, I'll help. Just don't do anything rash. Deal?" I nod and lean my head on her shoulder.

"Deal," I said. "Thank you for not thinking I'm crazy." She laughed.

"You're far from crazy," she said kissing my forehead. "Are you feeling better?"

"Somewhat. I'm sorry I woke you up."

"Don't apologize. It's me and you against the world remember? You're stuck with me too you know?" she said, and I laughed softly.

"I love you, Ally," I hadn't meant to say it, but after I said it, I knew I meant it. She leaned forward, forcing me to lean against the wall, so she could look at me.

"Do you really mean that?"

"With every fiber in my being," I say confidently, and she smiled.

"I love you, Leo," she said, and she leaned forward to kiss me, and I stopped her.

"I don't recommend that right now," I said, and she laughed. "Let me brush my teeth first." She nodded and stood up, turning off the shower. She helped me to my feet, and I brushed my teeth as she went back to bed. I checked my watch, it was 8:30 AM. I went to join her back in bed.

"Now," I said, kissing her softly. "That's better."

"Yes, it is," she says and kisses me again.

CHAPTER 10

My mind was still racing with everything. What if they had forced me into the military before the experiment? What if the surface was habitable? Why would they keep us down here? If my dream was accurate I'm betting the fences and everything was to protect the entrance to this shelter. But why? It doesn't make any sense.

"You up for eating?" she asked. "Or you still not feeling too hot?"

"I could probably eat something small," I said. "Toast sounds good. At least till my stomach figures out what it's doing." Though I knew that my stomach was fine, now that I had gotten over seeing my dad like that. I still didn't like it, but the initial shock was what made me sick and that was over. I don't think I'll ever get that image out of my head, even if I find out it was just a dream.

"Come on," she said and tugged on my hand to get out of bed with her. I drug myself up with her. "Get dressed and I'll meet you outside in ten minutes?" I nod and lean down to kiss her.

She disappears out the door and I look through my closet. Just grabbing the first things that caught my eye and put them on.

Ten minutes later, I'm leaning against Ally's door frame in the hallway. She opens it, gasps and jumps.

"You scared the hell out of me," she said laughing, I smile. We go to the elevator headed for the food level.

"I'd like to go to the library again sometime today," I say lightly, she nods. I figured computer records could be easily tampered with but books were a little harder to mess with. Granted you could just take them off the shelf, but I wanted to find more out on nuclear bombs and what they do. Mostly, I was looking for how long it would take the earth to recover and be habitable again, or at least enough for humans to survive up there. Given the state of the people I saw in my dreams, they were surviving, but not really living up there. I needed answers, if I could find them in the library, so be it. If all the books have been removed, then I know something is going on.

"We can go after we eat," Ally said, pulling me out of my thoughts.

"Okay gorgeous," I reply, and she smiled. We find some breakfast in the food court and sit down to eat. I'm not super hungry, but I eat so she won't worry about me. Afterwards, we head up to the library. "I'm gonna wander over here for a bit." I nodded towards the non-fiction side. "I'll come find you in our corner in a while okay?" She nodded and gave me a kiss before we went our separate ways.

I wander the aisles looking for anything on nuclear war. Or even war in general. I look through the reference books and the aisle after aisle of general non-fiction. After two and a half hours and walking every aisle on that side of the library, the only thing I could find to any kind of nuclear bomb was a small paragraph in a book about the mid-20th century that referenced the Cold War. Nothing on nuclear winter, nothing on the effects of nuclear radiation, nothing on anything that would have happened during the War. Something was obviously going on. They were lying to us.

I went to the other side of the library looking for Ally. I found her in our corner after a bit. She was reading some romance novel. I leaned down and kissed her.

"Find what you were looking for?" she asked.

"No," I say, putting more meaning into the word than was actually said. She nodded.

"I'm up for a nap. Or maybe a shower," she said, standing up.

"Sounds good to me, baby," I say and take her hand as we head back to the elevator.

The doors open and none other than Balding Joe is standing there. We step in and I nod at him. He nods back and I reach over to hit our floor button, but I stop. There's a key sticking out right next to the G button. Joe lunges forward and takes it out.

"Can't leave that laying around, can I?" he jokes nervously and puts the key in his pocket. I hit our floor button and glance over at Ally who raises an eyebrow at me. I match her look and we both face forward as we wait for our floor. The doors finally open.

"Have a good one, Joe," I say as we exit the elevator, he waves as the doors close again. Once inside my quarters, I kick off my shoes, trying to act nonchalant for anyone listening. Ally and I both head into the bathroom and turn on the shower. I shut the door as she sits on the counter, I start pacing back and forth.

"I couldn't find anything in reference to nuclear weapons," I start. "Nothing about anything that would have happened during the war. And then Balding Joe being up on the surface? He told me himself during my tour that that level requires a key, so nobody wanders up there accidently. He wasn't in any hazmat suit or anything, so obviously it's a building up there or the surface really is sustainable again. Otherwise he would die or get radiation poisoning or something right?"

"Yes," Ally said slowly, watching me pace. "If it was still radioactive up there, he could be affected. The problem is I'm not sure how long it would be radioactive after a nuclear bomb or how close we are to any of the bombing sites."

"Neither do I," I say. "Know any scientist buddies we could trust?"

"Unfortunately, no," she said. "I'm not sure we can trust anyone at this point. Not even Miss Anna when you're talking to her later, by the way."

"Shit," I said. "I forgot about her. How are we supposed to figure out what's going on if we can't trust anyone, I'm being tracked, and we need a key to get to the surface?"

"Relax, Leo," Ally said, getting off the sink and stopping my pacing. "We will figure this out. But it's not gonna be an overnight thing. This is only you're second full day of being out of the experiment. It took them longer than that to put it together, so it's gonna take longer to figure it out. Ok?" I sighed.

"I guess you're right," I lean back against the door. "It's just so frustrating to know that we're being lied to, again, but not being able to figure it out…. Wait. What's on the first floor?"

"I don't know," she said. "I've never been up there. I was always told its just what's needed to run the facility. Why?"

"That's what Joe told me too," I said. "But we didn't go up there. I wonder if that's really what's there…"

"Okay," she said lightly. "I think we're getting too far into the conspiracy theories. I agree that there's something going on and that we will get to the bottom of it. But you need to take a breath. Next you're going to start saying that we're alien clones."

"Well…" I joked and she smiled.

"Stop it."

"Yes, ma'am. Though I do need to figure out what to tell Miss Anna before she shows up later."

"Hmm," she mused. "I don't think you should tell her about the military dreams, in case they are real. Otherwise, they might try to wipe your memory again, because I highly doubt, they wanted you to remember all that. Given that they haven't mentioned it and it's not in your file or anything. If it is real, that is."

"It felt just like the other memories that have come back," I counter.

"I'm not saying I don't believe you Leo," she said calmly. "I'm just saying there is always the possibility that they messed around in your head a little too much." She raised her voice as I started to protest. "Not that we aren't going to look into it. Relax, will you?" she laughed and kissed me lightly.

"I don't like being lied to," I say flatly, but kissing her back.

"I'm well aware that you don't like being lied to," she said just as flatly. "You've always been that way. Trying to throw a surprise party for you was terrible." I laughed.

"You threw me a surprise party?"

"We tried, me and your parents. But you knew we were lying about something and you figured it out. I kept telling you to leave it alone, and you were stubborn as all hell." I laughed again.

"Well that obviously hasn't changed," I said with a smirk. "I'm not going to let this go."

"And I'm not telling you too," she said calmly. "I'm just asking you to take a break and think it through before you go charging into things and get yourself into trouble. They've obviously went through a lot to cover whatever this is, so you can't just go charging in. They're going to silence you one way or another. So, we have to be smart about it and not stubborn, got it?"

"Yes ma'am," I say, and she hits my chest.

"Now, come on," she said reaching over and shutting off the shower. "I'm going to give you a massage, and maybe you'll relax."

"I won't complain about that," I say slyly, she grabbed lotion from under the bathroom sink as I opened the door.

"I thought not," she said, and I laughed. "Take your shirt off and lay on your stomach."

"Trying to get me undressed," I said. "Shame on you." I laughed and she smirked and just pointed to the bed. "Okay, okay." I pulled my shirt over my head and laid down on the bed on my stomach. She came over and straddled my ass. She put some lotion in her hands, rubbed them together and began massaging my back. I moaned.

"Oh, I could get used to this," I said enjoying it.

"You used to be," she said working on a knot in my right shoulder. "We used to give each other massages all the time. That was probably the last time you had one it seems like." I laughed.

"I don't remember ever having one, so probably," I said and twisted my head around some to look at her with a smirk. "Did you have to take your shirt off too?" She pushed my head back into the pillow.

"Maybe, maybe not," she said, and I could hear her smile.

"Leaving a guy hanging," I sighed dramatically.

"You keep that up and that's all you're gonna get."

"Ouch," I said. "So, mean." She pushed hard in the center of my back, which actually hurt. "Okay, okay, I give up."

"Good boy." We both laughed. She continued to work on my back, shoulders, even my arms.

"You are an angel," I said dreamily, and she laughed. "This feels amazing."

"Good," she said. "You obviously needed it, too. You're so tense."

"I'm a tense guy," I said, and she laughed.

I must have fallen asleep, because the next thing I knew I was woken up by a knock at the door. I looked around as I got off the bed, Ally was gone. I didn't have any new dreams or memories while I slept. I'm assuming Ally had me so relaxed that I slept hard. I opened the door and there stood Miss Anna and Ryan behind her.

"Ryan?" I said, kind of taken aback. She smiled at me and looked down. I looked down too and realized I still wasn't wearing a shirt. "Shit. I'm sorry, come in." I walked back over to the bed and pulled my shirt back on. They both came in and I pulled both the chairs from my table and brought them closer to my desk. Miss Anna took her usual spot in my desk chair and Ryan sat in the other chair. I sat down slowly. Completely unsure of how this was going to go, yet I couldn't help glancing at Ryan.

"So, Leo," Miss Anna said after she got out her trusty pad and pen. "As you can see, I've brought a guest today." I laughed nervously and cleared my throat.

"I can see that," I said lightly.

"And how do you feel about that?"

"Honestly," I said. "Panic. I know you said that you would try to get her here so I could talk to her, but honestly I thought it was going to be later than right now."

"I can leave if you'd like," Ryan said.

"No," I said. "Stay. Honestly, it's good to see you. My emotions are just all over the place since I found out that you knew about this whole thing the whole time. That you were lying to me."

"It was just a job, Leo," she said dismissively.

"But it wasn't to me," I shot back, getting angry already. "I cared about you, hell, I probably could have even fell in love with you had I not been pulled out when I was. But it was just a job to you?" She sighed.

"I cared about you, Leo," she said slowly. "You were my friend, but it wouldn't have gone farther than that. I knew you were going towards that, that's why I told Joe to pull you out soon. I didn't want to have to break your heart like that." There was calmness in her voice that was unnerving. It reminded me of

Balding Joe.

"So that just makes you so noble?" I'm struggling to keep my voice level. "That you broke my heart as a friend instead of a boyfriend? That just makes it better, huh? Guess what, it doesn't make it better for me. You know how much I hate being lied to—well hell, I don't know if you know that. I don't even know how long we've known each other or how well we know each other. A couple days ago, I thought I knew you like the back of my hand, but now? You might as well be a stranger to me."

"Please don't be like that, Leo," she said softly. "I was hoping we could still be friends. Maybe not as close as we were but—"

"How long have we known each other?" I ask, cutting her off.

"Why does it matter?" she asked. "You obviously just wanted me here to berate me, not to work anything out."

"Because I want to hear at least one honest thing from you," I say, ignoring her other comment.

"I—" she shot a look at Miss Anna, I saw Anna shake her head out of the corner of my eye. "I don't know. I'd have to check your file." I know that that look had to have something to do with whatever cover up is happening, but I told Ally I wouldn't just go charging in, so I don't address it.

"You'd have to check my file?" I ask sarcastically, I'm out of my chair, pacing behind it. "If we're such good friends, Ryan, how come you can't tell me how long we've known each other? If you really wanted to continue being my friend, you'd think you'd remember how long we have been friends to begin with."

"I'm sorry you feel that way, Leo," she said looking at her hands in her lap. I sighed, standing behind my chair, I place my hands on the back of it and lean over it.

"Part of me will always care for you, Ryan," I said quietly. "I can't just shut off what I thought was ten years of friendship. I can't just shut off those feelings that I developed over that time. But I don't trust you, and trust means everything to me. So, until I believe that I can trust you again, then, no, we can't continue to be friends."

"I'm sorry to hear that, Leo," she said as she stood up. Part of me thought she really meant that. The other part was still annoyed with the calmness of her voice. "I wish you the best and hope that it will change in the future." I stared at my hands on the back of my chair as she walked to the door and left without another word. I stood there silent for a bit, my brain racing, my emotions going crazy.

"Leo?" Miss Anna said, and I looked at her. "Do you want to talk about what just happened?" I sighed again.

"No offense Miss Anna," I said softly. "But not really, not right now. I really just want to go work out and try to process it all. Can we pick this up tomorrow?"

"That's quite alright honey," she said, packing up her pen and pad. "Same time tomorrow, I promise no more visitors." She smiled and I laughed a little as she headed for the door.

"Thanks, Miss Anna." She left and I changed into workout clothes. I walked out my door and automatically headed down to Ally's. I knocked and she opened it after a minute with a smile that quickly faded when she saw my face.

"You okay?" she asked as I walked in.

"I really don't want to talk about it right now," I said, trying to not sound rude. "But I am going to go work out, I didn't know if you wanted to come with me or not?"

"Do you want me to come with you? Or would you rather be alone?" she didn't sound angry or hurt by it, genuinely concerned for what I wanted.

"I want you to come," I said softly. "Just being around you makes me feel better. I'll talk to you about it later. I just need some time to sweat and workout all this... stuff going on right now."

"We'll just work out," she said. "I promise. Give me a minute to get changed." I paced by her bed, too antsy to sit down and wait. A couple minutes later, she came out of the bathroom workout ready. "Let's go."

I follow her out the door and to the elevator. I take her hand as we wait for the doors to open on B2. She squeezes my hand, a simple gesture, but it's reassuring. We make our way to the workout room and I hop on a treadmill. She gets on the one next to me. We run for a while, just running. My body is working while my brain is still racing. Part of me feels bad for how I treated Ryan, the part that still cares about her. The other part thinks I was too soft on her. Either way, I probably won't be seeing her again any time soon. And that look between her and Miss Anna? Was that because I wasn't in the experiment for as long as I thought? Or had Miss Anna coached her on what to say, to break my attachment of her?

I get off the treadmill and head to the weights, setting up a bench press with 75 pounds on each side. I lay down and I see Ally come over and stand above me, spotting me. I smile and take the bar off the rack.

After a while on the weights, my brain has slowed down and some of my muscles are shaking. I lay back on the floor after doing sit ups and Ally looks at me.

"You good?" she asked smiling and I laughed a little, still catching my breath.

"I'm okay," I say in between breaths. "I think I'm done though."

"You sure two and a half hours is enough?" she teased me.

"Damn," I said looking at my watch. "Has it really been that long? I'm sorry." She laughed and helped me to my feet. "I'm ready for a shower."

"You need one," she teased again, and I laughed.

"You don't smell so hot yourself baby," I say poking her in the side as we reach the elevator.

We make it back to our floor and Ally walks past my door.

"Let me grab some clothes and I'll be right there," she said, and I went into my quarters, leaving the door cracked so she could get in. I sat down on my bed to take my shoes off, some of my muscles still twitching from overuse. I sat there for a minute with my head in my hands. I didn't hear Ally come in, but I felt her take my hand away from my face and lead me into the bathroom. She closed the door.

"I really do want to take a shower, but I wanted to talk too," she said. "Turn around." She smiles as I groan and twirls her finger in the air, indicating me to turn around. I do and I can hear her taking off her clothes.

"You really just love to torture me, don't you?" I ask, still facing the wall. She laughs.

"It is a fun time for me," she said lightly, and laughed again. I hear her pull back the shower curtain and get in, turning on the water as she did. "Okay." I turn and of course, she's already in the shower and I can't see anything. "So, tell me what happened earlier."

I run through everything that happened with Ryan and the whole conversation, including the look between her and Miss Anna. Ally poked her head out from behind the curtain.

"Well no wonder you were upset," she said. "Though I agree, I think that look that they shared has something to do with the cover up that's going on. I feel like she remembered how long you guys have known each other but was told not to tell you."

"So, she's still lying to me. Great," I say bitterly.

"In all fairness," she said softly. "You don't know if they have threatened her or something to make sure she doesn't tell you anything." I raised my eyebrow at her, and she pulled her head back behind the curtain.

"I never thought I would hear you defending her," I said, teasing.

"I'm not," she said. "I still feel like she's competition. But given all that they've done to keep this quiet, I wouldn't doubt they would do or say something to her to keep her quiet."

"She's not competition," I replied. "Not anymore at least. If I never would have found out she was lying, she might have still been. But now that I know, that ship has sailed, permanently. But I do agree with you. They probably did threaten her or something to make sure she doesn't talk. So where does that leave us?"

"Unfortunately, still with a lot of circumstantial evidence," she said. "We need some hard evidence. And I think the only way we are going to be able to get some, is to take some risks. As much as I don't want to."

"How do you mean?"

"Turn around," she said, and I did. She shut off the water and got out of the shower. "Your turn." I pulled off my shirt without thinking about it and turned around. She had a towel wrapped around her. "Good try."

"I wasn't trying," I said almost innocently and grinned. She squeezed past me and faced the wall.

"Uh huh, sure," she said. "Hurry up." I pulled off the rest of my clothes and got in the shower myself turning the water back on.

"So, what kind of risks are we talking?" I said, getting back on track. As much as I would love to flirt, I wanted to get to the bottom of this whole situation first.

"I think we need to see what's on the first floor to start with," she said, and I poked my head out to look at her. She was in her bra and underwear and I froze for a second. She looked at me and I panicked and pulled my head back.

"Shit. Sorry," I said. "I was just surprised that you suggested that."

"Well, the part you aren't going to like," she started. "Is that it's got to be me to go up there." I didn't care at this point, I stuck my head back out. She shot me a look, which I ignored, and put her hands on her hips.

"You're not serious?" I said.

"I told you, you weren't going to like it," she replied. "And do you mind?" I glared but pulled my head back again.

"Well of course I don't like it," I said. "That's putting you at risk. I don't want you to get in trouble or get hurt."

"Yes," she said lightly. "I get that. But you're being tracked. I can at least move about the place without causing too many issues. I can go up there tonight."

"And what happens if you get caught?" I retort.

"Well," she said. "I'm a pretty good flirt…" I poked my head out and look at her again. She's fully dressed now and sitting on the counter.

"What if it's a girl?" I countered and she shrugged and laughed. "If I wasn't so focused on making sure you're not hurt I would be really turned on right now." She laughed again.

"I may have done some experimenting in the experiment," she said lightly, I just kind of stared at her. "But at least it's a plan if something happens." I shake my head, finishing my shower.

"And what if it doesn't work?" I say as I shut off the water and open the curtain. I see her look down and blush. I'm not concerned right now.

"You've grown a little since the last time I saw you," she said slyly and it's my turn to blush. I grab a towel and wrap it around my waist. "I was enjoying the show." She giggled.

"What happens if it doesn't work?" I said bringing her back to the conversation and trying to stay focused myself. She sighed.

"I'll be fine," she said and gave me a look. "I can take care of myself remember?" It was my turn to sigh.

"I don't like it, but I guess it's our only option," I muse. "Unless we want to wait another week and a half till I'm cleared, and I get rid of this thing?" I hold up my wrist, showing my tracker.

"I don't think you'll last that long," she said laughing.

"Ok, that's fair." I laugh too. "I'm too curious to wait that long."

"Exactly," she said, and kissed me. "Now get dressed and we can go get food."

"You and food," I said, laughing. I open the door and head to my closet as she sits on the bed. I take my towel off, because why not? She's already seen it. I hear a cat call whistle behind me, and I throw my towel at her. She laughs and I get dressed.

We go down to the food level and eat, I'm still thinking about this 'plan.' It doesn't sound like much of a plan, but it's all we have for now. I hate the idea of putting her in harms way, but she is right, I'm being tracked. After we eat, she pulls me back to the elevator.

"Come on," she says and then leans in to whisper, "You owe me a massage." I smirk and she laughs.

"I'm down for that," I said, we got on the elevator and I hit our floor button.

"I thought you would be."

Back in my room, I grab the lotion from the bathroom. I say, "Take your shirt off and lay down on your stomach." I smirk, repeating what she said. To my surprise, she peels off her shirt in front of me and reaches around to undo her bra. She throws both on the floor and I'm entranced by her breasts, which are beautiful. She laughs and goes and lays down on my bed on her stomach. I clear my throat and follow her. I straddle her butt like she did me and put some lotion in my hands. I started rubbing her back, while simultaneously trying not to listen to her moans.

About fifteen minutes in, I'm having a hard time keeping myself in check. I'm hard and I swear that she's rubbing her ass against me. It takes me a minute to realize that she actually is rubbing her ass against me. I lean down and bite her ear.

"You're doing that on purpose," I growl in her ear and she giggles. She manages to roll over under me and pulls me in for a kiss. She takes the kiss deeper and I throw caution to the wind, taking her breasts in my hands. She moans into my mouth as I pinch her nipples softly. The taste of her tongue on mine is intoxicating. I pull back just to bite her neck and trace my tongue from her neck down to her right nipple. I suck it into my mouth and nibble lightly on it. She moans louder and pulls my face harder onto her breast. I pull back long enough to pull my shirt over my head, before diving back in and repeating the process on her left nipple. She's scratching up my back making me moan.

I kiss my way slowly down her stomach, licking her belly button, making her giggle. My hands slowly undo the button on her jeans, and I slide them and her underwear down. I kiss my way further down as I pulled her bottoms off completely. I kiss down her left thigh, to her calf and then back up her right leg. She's moaning louder, I can tell she wants me on her sex. I lean into it and gently lick her clit once. She growls, because I'm teasing her. I smile up at her, before I take her clit into my mouth and suck on it. I finger her at the same time. Her hips are moving in motion with me, riding my face as I eat her out.

Her moans are getting still louder and her breath racing. I know she's getting close. I pick up the pace, finger fucking her and abusing her clit with my mouth. She screams loudly as she finally climaxes. She collapses, trying to catch her breath. I get off the bed, smiling down at her, long enough to take my pants and underwear off.

"You're good at that," she said between breaths, smirking.

"Just wait, baby," I say softly smirking as well, getting between her knees again and leaning down to kiss her hard. Her hands claw at my back, pulling me closer. The moment I enter her, both of our breathes catch and we moan together.

"Fuck," I say under my breath and she laughs. "God. You were worth waiting for." She grins and pulls me in for a kiss again as I start moving slowly.

CHAPTER 11

Later, I wake up naked in my bed, but alone. I look at my bracelet, it's just after midnight. I know that she probably went to go check out the first floor. I'm reminiscing about earlier when I realize that she probably did that to make sure I wouldn't stop her from going to the first floor. I laugh and shake my head to myself. I can't complain. She was amazing and she wore me out for sure. She knew I would fall asleep. Part of me was mad at her for seducing me just to get me to fall asleep. But the bigger part enjoyed it too much to complain.
I got up because I had to pee, came back and pulled on some shorts, sat on the edge of the bed. I wonder how long she has been gone already, I'm starting to get worried. I contemplate going after her, but I am being tracked and that would draw too much unnecessary attention to her. I'm too antsy, so I start pacing by my bed again.

After about thirty minutes, there's a knock at my door. I race over and pulled it open. Ally is standing there, I can tell something happened by the look on her face. I take her hand and drag her inside, directly to the bathroom. I shut the door and turn on the shower.

"What happened?" I asked automatically.

"Well, after you fell asleep," she started. "I decided to go up to the first floor. I dressed like I was going to work out, that way I can say I just hit the wrong button if someone was right there, you know? Anyway, I get up there and it's a hallway like this floor, but each room is labeled. 'Maintenance,' 'Sewage,' 'Recycling.' What you would expect. I get further down to the 'Records' room. I go in there and there's filing cabinets everywhere. I look for the P's and find your file. It turns out you weren't put directly into the experiment. You spent a couple of years above ground with the military, patrolling and protecting the entrance. Then it says you had 'personal issues,' so they wiped your memory again and put you in the experiment."

"'Personal issues?'" I asked. "It didn't say what that means?"

"Nope. Just 'personal issues,'" she said watching me pacing again. "But you were right! You were in the military for a while. I'm assuming they reset your memory completely before they put you up there though, to make you a more obedient soldier. But now that they took the implant out some of those memories are coming back instead of just the before ones."

"What happened next?"

"I left that room and tried a few more, most of them were locked. But there was one that had all these maps and things in it, I didn't really understand it. But they were definitely maps of the surface and there were places marked on them. I couldn't tell if they were marked for troops or people living up there, but there's something up there. There's no doubt about it. Holy shit."

"I know," I said still pacing.

"After that I headed back to the elevator and ran into someone who was getting off the elevator. I just told him I hit the wrong button and didn't realize it until I got off. I don't think he thought anything of it. He just kind of nodded and walked away. How are we going to get out of here?"

"I don't know," I said. "But one thing is for sure, I gotta get this tracker off me before we try anything."

"We could always just cut you hand off," she suggested.

"Ha ha," I said. "I'm still mad at you for seducing me so I wouldn't stop you from going up there." She grinned.

"Oh, like you didn't like it?"

"I didn't say that," I said, and she laughed.

"That's what I thought," she smirked. "I've heard that if they're tampered with, they send an alarm to the people who run the place."

"That's what I figured," I said looking at it. It was tight, but movable. "We might be able to slip it off?"

"We'd need something slippery," she said, getting off the counter to look under the sink. "Soap?"

"We can try it," I said. We put my hand over the sink and cover it in soap and try to slide the bracelet off. It hurts like hell, but after working it for a bit, we're able to slip it off my hand completely. I wipe it and my hand off on a towel. I rub my hand and can tell it's going to be sore for a bit.

"Okay," she said. "We can put it on your bed, since it's still late." She opens the door and tosses the bracelet on my bed, closing the door again.

"Now we go up to the first floor and find a way up to the surface," I said. "There's got to be another way other than the elevator." I looked down, I was still in just my shorts. "First I have to get dressed and you need to go change too. Something movable, because we're probably going to have to run at some point."

Ally leaves to change and I get dressed quietly, given they probably think I'm sleeping. Five minutes later we're both in the hall headed for the elevator. My heart is thumping in my chest, but I'm doing my best to remain calm. We hit B1 and hold our breath that there is no one there when the doors open, there isn't. We walk down the hallway, I'm reading door signs as we go. I try few doors as we go, all locked. We get down to the one marked 'security,' I open it slowly. Lucky for us, the one guy in the room is asleep, leaned back in his chair, his feet on the desk. The desk has multiple screens all showing cameras from around the facility.

I look at him again, he is carrying a gun on his hip and he has a set of keys on his belt. I look at Ally and point to these things. She cocks her head and I look around for something to knock this guy out with. We can't risk him waking up and hitting some alarm. There's a fire extinguisher on the wall. I take it down and hit the guy on the head with it. He falls out of his chair and doesn't get up.

"What did you do that for?" Ally asked as I reached down and got his gun and keys.

"I couldn't risk him hitting some alarm if we woke him," I said and stood looking at the screens again. "At least he is unconscious. It gives us more time." I don't see anyone else on this floor, I look down at the keys. There's a small gold one that looks like the one Balding Joe had in the elevator. "Do we wanna just try and go up the elevator?" I held up the key to her.

"Might as well," she said. "Go big or go home." We push the unconscious guy behind the door so he won't be seen right away if someone comes in. I tuck the gun in the back of my pants and put my shirt over it.

"You ready?" I say, looking at the cameras again to make sure nobody was outside the door. We were clear. I look at Ally.

"I'm ready," she said nodded at me, she had grabbed the guard's baton and had it behind her back. I open the door and lead the way back to the elevator, glancing behind us occasionally, making sure the guard hadn't woken up yet. The doors open and I pull the keys out as we get in. I find the key that I had shown Ally and try it in the slot by the G button, it turns easily. I push the button and the doors close.

I grab Ally's hand and pull out the gun with my other pointing it at the door. Ally has the baton in her free hand. The doors open and there's no one. I release Ally's hand and grip the gun tighter. I swing left and then right. Clear. I look around, lowering the gun a little. We're in a clean room by the looks of it, but there's weapons on the wall next to the other door. I walk over to the wall and grab a rifle checking to see that it's loaded and slinging it over my shoulder. I grab another pistol and put it in my pants. Ally is beside me loading up as well and I smile, knowing she's got my back if shit hits the fan.

We're loaded down with weapons and we turn to face the doors, no idea what is behind them. I take a deep breath and push them open with my rifle leading the way. We're in a dark empty hallway. I pick a direction and walk softly. Ally is behind me. We reached the end and there's another door. Beside this one, gas masks line the wall. I grab one and hand it to Ally. Putting one on myself, checking to make sure hers is on before I open the door. Just because my dream showed the surface livable it doesn't mean it is. Better safe than sorry. I opened the door and felt the cool breeze from outside. It was dark, but I could make out other buildings around this one.

As soon as I stepped foot out of the door, the alarms and lights went off. The guard was probably awake.

"Run!" I yell at Ally. I take off towards what I hope is the fence. There are spotlights circling, but it's still hard to see in this darkness. I hug tightly to a building and stop for a second, trying to figure out which way to go. I see people moving further ahead of us. They're looking for us. Left, more buildings and further darkness. Right, I can almost make out the fence. These masks don't make it any easier to see, but I decide right is the way to go.

"Come on," I say to Ally and point towards the right in case she can't hear me. We head in that direction, making it a point to avoid the spotlights. I can hear shouting on either side of us. I can see the fence ahead of us now, yes. I'm sure of it. We finally make it to the fence line. Unfortunately, there's no gate, we're going to have to climb it. I look at Ally and point up. Getting into position to give her a leg up. She nods and steps onto my knee to begin climbing the fence. She reaches the top and easily lands on her feet on the other side. I jump and climb the fence myself and feel the light hit my back as I'm doing so. I hear shouting and footfalls heading our way. I try to climb faster, and I see Ally holding her rifle pointing it behind me, waiting. I finally reach the top and jump down beside her.

"Let's go!" I said, tugging on her arm as I take off in the opposite direction of the fence. We run and run and run. I take a chance and glance behind us. I can see the fence and the light behind it, but it's further away now. It doesn't look like anyone is following us. I still can't see very well, but my eyes have adjusted enough to make out some of what we're running over. It looks like grass for the most part, spread out and a lot of dirt. I look ahead of us and I can see some large shapes. I'm assuming they're buildings. I grab Ally's arm to slow her down. I point ahead of us to the buildings.

"I think we can rest up there," I said loudly. "It doesn't look like they're following us." She nods, and we slow to a walk, heading towards the structures. The closer we get I realize they are houses or what is left of houses. There are a few that are mostly intact, but the majority are pretty much destroyed. I'm assuming we were far enough from the bombing site that most of the damage is just from 70 years of neglect. Any closer and the houses wouldn't here at all, or at least that's what I thought. We head to the closest one that is mostly intact, and Ally stops. I look at her and she's staring at the house.

"You don't recognize it?" she asks. I look again, even cock my head to the side, like it's going to help. Then it comes back to me.

"Holy shit," I say. "This was my house."

"It looks good," she said. "Given it's been through a nuclear war." I laugh and walk up to the front door, or what should have been the front door. It was gone, I stepped through the threshold. Ally walks in beside me and we look around. The roof is missing on the left side, but the right is mostly intact. I walk further in still looking around. The problem is, I still don't remember most of this. Ally can see that I look confused and she grabs my hand and leads me further into the house. We go down some broken stairs into the basement. She takes me through another door, and I see what I recognize as my room. I step past her and see my bed with my nightstand where I pulled out my class ring for Ally. My room looks practically untouched. I sit on the bed. Ally comes over and stands between my knees. I lean my head against her stomach, and she runs her fingers through my hair.

"We got out," I said, still talking loudly, given the mask.

"I knew we would," she said. "We should try to get some sleep. We need to look for supplies in the morning." I nod and stand. I start pulling weapons off me and out of my pockets setting most of them on the nightstand. I put a pistol under my pillow and lay down, as Ally does the same.

"I hate these masks," I said bitterly.

"I know," she said, entwining her fingers with mine. "But we need to keep them on until we know if it's safe to breath or not." She pulls the tattered blankets up over us.

"I know," I said. I fall asleep fairly easily, given everything that has happened.

I wake up a few hours later and blink my eyes against the light. Then I realize that the light is the sun coming in through the broken windows near the ceiling. I sit up and just feel the sun for a minute. I look over and realize that I'm alone and panic starts to rise in my chest. I grab the pistol from under my pillow and jump out of bed.

"Ally!" I yell as loud as I can as I walked down the hall, back towards the stairs. "Ally! Where are you?"

"Here," I hear her shout, it's coming from above me. I run up the stairs with the gun still ahead of me. I reach the landing by the door and look outside, it's sunny and warm. I turn and continue up the stairs.

"Ally?" I say again.

"I'm right here," she said from behind me. I turn and lower my gun. She's not wearing her mask and I'm assuming she could see the panic in my eyes. "It's okay babe. I apparently took it off in my sleep, but I'm breathing fine. No problems." I put my gun back in my pants and slowly took off my mask too. I took a deep breath and nothing. I was fine.

"No problems," I agree softly, I hook my mask on my belt. I'm not ready to just leave it behind yet and it might come in handy. "What are you doing up here anyway?"

"Come here," she says as she turns through another doorway and I follow. It's the kitchen, the same one my dad said he was going to beat up Ally's foster dad in. Ally stops behind the counter and I see all the stuff she's collected. Water bottles, lighters, canned food, knives.

"You've been busy," I said looking it all over.

"I've searched most of the upstairs," she replies. "Though there's a safe upstairs that I can't get into. Any idea what the combination is?" I laugh.

"I barely remember anything," I said, and she laughed too.

"That's fair," she said. "But I figured I'd ask. It might be something simple that you do remember. I'm gonna go search downstairs now that you're awake. You wanna go take a look?"

"Sure baby," I said and leaned in to kiss her. "Just don't go far."

"Yes sir," she mocked, and I shot her a look, she laughed.

She went towards the stairs that I just came up from and I headed down the hall. First door was a bathroom, a small one. Second door was an office I could see what was left of a desk and computer. Third was a bedroom, pink walls and a big A on the wall. I realized that it was my little sister's room. I wasn't necessarily surprised that my parents kept it this way after she died, but it still hit me harder than I thought it would. I closed the door and headed towards the last one. My parents room. It was simple, there was a broken bed and night stands on both sides. A dresser against the wall, also broken. I go to the door in the corner assuming that they would keep the safe in their closet. Sure enough, there it was in the corner.

I kneel down in front of it trying to think of what my parents would use as the combination. I tried both of their birthdays first, then mine. Finally, I got it with Amanda's birthday. The safe clicked open and I looked inside. Two shotguns and a few pistols, as well as a lot of ammunition. I grab a bag that's in the closet with me and load it all in there. I take it all back to the kitchen with me and on the way back I spot a picture on the floor that was hanging in the hallway. It was my parents, Ally, and I all around a birthday cake. Ally was in the middle, I'm assuming it was her birthday. I picked it up and took it out of the broken frame. I wanted something to remember them by. I walked into the kitchen and there was a person standing there. I dropped the bag and picture and pulled my pistol from my pants.

CHAPTER 12

"Who are you?" I said firmly, pistol pointed at them. They are facing away from me and have their hood up, so I have no clue. They put their hands slowly up and turn around to face me. They have a scarf covering their mouth, but I can tell it's a woman by her soft eyes. She lowers one of her hands to pull down her scarf. I hear Ally coming up the stairs behind me.

"Ally," I say. "We got company." I hear a thud and she's by my side in a flash, but she doesn't point her gun at the woman. I focus my attention on her again and realize she looks familiar, but I can't be sure who she is.

"Carol?" Ally said and I faulter and lower my gun.

"Carol?" I say. "As in my mother Carol?" I'm looking between Ally and the woman. She does look like my mother, but the only memory I have of her right now is of when I was twelve.

"Ally?" she said, she sounded like my mother too, but older. "Leo?" I cock my head to the side.

"You'll have to forgive him, Carol," Ally said. "He still doesn't remember everything, yet." She walks over and hugs the woman.

"I figured they would do that to you guys," Carol said as she pulled away from Ally and looked at me. "I am your mother, Leo. I heard there had been an escape from the shelter and had to come see if it was you or not." She saw the bag on the floor with the things from the safe. "I see you remember your sister's birthday." I put my gun on the counter, still not approaching her, but curious.

"I tried yours and Dad's first and my own," I said. "It was the only one left."

"You've grown into a handsome man," she said, I could see tears forming in her eyes. She stepped towards me and I let her hug me. I hugged her back awkwardly, knowing she was my mother and remembering she was were two different things. She pulled back and kissed my cheek. "You look so much like your father. He would be so proud of you."

"Where is he?" Ally asked the question that I didn't want the answer to.

"He never made it out of the cryo-tubes," my mother said, and I breathed a sigh of relief. She looked at me weird.

"He had a dream," Ally started for me as I placed my hands on the counter and breathed for a minute. "That he had killed Matt when he was in the military."

"No, honey," Mom said. "No, he died in his sleep. There were a lot of people who didn't make it out of the tubes." Ally rubbed my back as I composed myself.

"So, what happened? After the sirens went off? Getting here? Everything," I said. My mom turned and sat at one of the chairs. Ally sat on the counter and I leaned against it next to her.

"Your father had forgotten his wallet," Mom said. "So, we were already heading back here when they went off. I wanted to hurry and get back to our shelter, the one you went to, so we could be with you. But your father wanted us to go to the nearest one. So, we did and good thing too. The bombs started as soon as they closed the doors. They kept us there for a week or so before they started freezing everyone. They promised they would wake us together. And they did, well they tried. I woke up to them trying to revive your father."

"He obviously couldn't be revived," she continued. "But they told me it had been over 60 years and that they had determined that the surface was safe, but it wasn't necessarily livable. So, they allowed us to go up, but we could go back down anytime we wanted. Kind of like a revolving door. The first thing I asked was about you and the other shelters. They said that a handful of the shelters had closed ranks, keeping their people below ground, only allowing military topside. Apparently, the important people decided that this was the best time to raise a more 'obedient and controllable' generation."

"Your shelter was one of them," she said bitterly. "They said that your shelter had cut off communications with everyone else and had set up a perimeter topside to keep people from trying to break the rest of them out. We've tried a couple times, but they just have too much firepower."

"So, they lied to us and kept us under there to raise us like cattle?" I say disgusted. "After they had woken us up, I asked about you and Dad and they said that you hadn't made it to a shelter." I knew that much from my letter.

"We made it, alright," Mom said softly. "Luckily to one of the ones that wasn't controlled by the power-hungry part of the military. I had heard that that was the plan for all of the shelters, but most of them realized that it was wrong and decided to ignore the orders they had gotten more than 60 years before, thankfully."

"It makes sense that that's what they would want to keep us for," Ally said. "Easier to have soldiers that don't ask questions. They could have told us that anyone of the surface was contaminated and had to be killed. They already had those masks by the door and we took them without question and the air is fine."

"In most places," Mom said. "There are still some places that isn't safe, so it's best to keep one with you anyway. Mostly around the craters from the original bombs."

"So you're still living in your shelter?" I asked.

"Unfortunately, no," Mom said sadly. "Some people decided they wanted it for themselves. They let those us who wanted to leave, leave, but killed all the military that was still there. Even though they were the whole reason we were alive. They have a lot of the weapons there too. That's why we didn't stand a chance getting into your shelter. But I'm living in the smaller city not far from here with other survivors. We make do. We can grow certain things and there's some animals still around."

"If you don't have weapons," I started. "How come you didn't take the ones out of the safe?"

"We have some weapons," she said. "Just not enough to take on a fortress like that. But I was keeping that for two reasons. One was in case you ever got out and I could see if it was really you. Two was a back up plan, in case anything went wrong with the other survivors and I needed to get out fast."

"What do you mean in case anything went wrong?" Ally asked, reading my mind.

"It's a very wild west type of place now," Mom said. "You try to make friends and trades, but when it really comes down to it, you can't trust anyone. Some people still have family and they keep close, but everyone else is pretty much on their own. We may all live in the city, but there's some there that would kill us all just to get what we have. It's sad really."

"Sounds like it," I said. "Why have you stayed?"

"I needed to know about you and Ally," she said. "I needed to know if you survived and if you would ever get out of there. I couldn't leave if there was even the possibility that you two were alive." I heard Ally sniffle. "Yes, Ally, even you. You were like a daughter to me and you've grown into a beautiful woman. And

I'm so glad to see you two together. I always knew you two would end up together." We both smiled and Ally squeezed my hand.

"So, what now, Mom?" I asked and she smiled. "I mean do we stay here, or do we move on?"

"I don't have a reason to stay here now that you two are out," she said. "So that part is up to you. I don't know if you have anyone you'd like to fight for down there?" I looked at Ally and she looked at me, in silent agreement.

"No," I said easily. "We're good. Where we going?"

"Well," she started. "I've heard that Australia and New Zealand weren't as effected by the War as the rest of the world. Kind of like a safe haven."

"That's like on the other side of the world," I said. "That would take a long time to get there."

"Yes," she said, standing up and pulling something out of her pocket. She spread it out on the table and it was a map of the world. Or what the world was before the War. "But we could do it. We could go up the coast to what was Alaska and go over to what was Russia. The ocean levels have receded, so there's land connecting them again. Or there should be. From there, down the Asian coast and we would have to take a boat to Australia. It's doable." She followed the line with her finger as she explained it.

"Wouldn't it just be easier to take a boat the whole way?" I ask.

"The problem with that is getting enough supplies to last us the trip. At least going on land, we can pick some up where we find them. Fuel, food, water, and anything we need."

"Makes sense," I said. "What do you think, babe?"

"It sounds like a good plan," Ally said. "Though we wouldn't be walking the whole way, would we? That could take years."

"I've been fixing up a car," Mom said. "It's working now but we'll just have to find fuel along the way. Or get different vehicles."

"I'm in," I said. "I've always wanted to go on an adventure."

"At least as far as you can remember?" Ally said teasing and I slapped her thigh, she laughed. "I'm in if you're in. I gotta keep you in line." We all laughed.

"Okay," Mom said, folding up her map. "That settles it. Let's pack up these supplies and go get my car. There should be some more bags in your closet Leo."

"Already got them," Ally said, hopping off the counter and picking up the things she had dropped earlier. She had grabbed all our weapons from my room as well. We packed up everything that she had found into three backpacks and one duffel bag. I had a strap across my chest with shotgun shells in it and a shot gun over my shoulder.

"I feel badass," I said, and Ally laughed.

"You look sexy," she said and kissed me, Mom groaned.

"Maybe I shouldn't bring you two along," she said and laughed.

"You're the one who said you knew we'd end up together," I counter.

"Okay," Mom said. "That's fair. So, we are still pretty close to the shelter and the fortress thing, so we have to keep it down when we leave. Understood?"

Ally and I both nod as we grab backpacks and I grab the duffel. We both have our masks tied to our belts. I packed one of my dad's jackets as well. It was a leather one that fit me well, it was a way to remember him as well as the picture I found. Mom led the way out of the house, heading the opposite of the way Ally and I had come in the night before. We walked for a good two hours, not talking and keeping our eyes open and weapons ready. Mom finally veered off the main road behind an old auto shop. She brought us around back and pulled up the garage door and there was a car, that looked old, yes, but it looked functional and that's what mattered.

"Meet Daisy," Mom said, and I laughed.

"Daisy?" I asked.

"Every car has to have a name," she said and shot me a look. Ally hit me and shot me a look too.

"I'm starting to second guess this," I said and they both laughed.

"Shot gun," Ally said, and Mom laughed.

"Now I'm definitely second guessing this," I said. We threw all our stuff in the back seat in case we needed to reach it in a hurry. I climbed in with the cargo and Ally and Mom got in the front. Mom started it up and slowly back out of the garage.

"I've already got all my stuff in the trunk," Mom said. "Been planning this for years, collecting extra water, food, or ammo when I could. At least not enough to be noticed though. The more people think you have, the more of a target you are." I was very impressed with my mother, to be alone for this long and be able to learn new things and how to survive.

"You've done well for yourself," Ally said, reading my mind again. "How long have you been out here?"

"I've been awake for about ten years," she said. "But it took them about two years before they wanted to take over the place. So, I've been out here for eight or so. It took me a bit to get used to it, to be honest. There were times where I didn't think I would survive." I could hear the pain in her voice. I felt bad for her. All these years out here without Dad.

"That must have been rough," Ally replied.

"It was for the first couple years," Mom said softly. "But I got through it, I had to. Otherwise out here, you'll die quick."

"I'm proud of you," I said from the backseat. "Dad would have been too." Mom smiled at me in the rearview mirror.

"Thank you, sweetie," she said. "That means a lot."

We rode along in silence for a while, I was watching out the window. Some places looked untouched and still as green as I remember them. Others were a barren wasteland. It's amazing how much damage we caused. I knew that the same kind of people who wanted to keep us locked away in a bunker would do this kind of destruction again. They just wanted power; they didn't care what they did to get it.

We got away from the smaller city where my mom was living and the green expanded more. I saw deer and bears along the road. Not affected by humans as much anymore, so they were able to roam freely. Obviously, the bombs had been focused on more populated areas, which made sense. It was amazing to see all the trees and high grass, not that I remembered much of it from before.

Ally and Mom were talking. Mom was asking about our time in the bunker, Ally explained about the day the sirens went off, being in the bunker, and the experiment. When she got to the part about Carl, I saw my mom squeezing her hand. She described seeing me both in the experiment and when I came out without my memories and our time since then.

"So, you don't remember everything yet?" Mom asked me, glancing at me in the rearview mirror.

"No," I sighed. "I get a lot of flashes mostly, memories here and there. I remember my fifth birthday party, you, Dad, and Mandy being there." I saw tears brim her eyes. "I remember Dad pushing me on a swing when I was young. I remember more about Ally and our time together. I remember when Dad went to beat up Jim and when I beat up that kid in high school." She laughed.

"You were so mad that your dad agreed that you should be suspended," she said smiling. "But he was right, and I agreed with him that that kid deserved it."

"He told us not to tell you that he was proud of me for doing it," I said smiling. She laughed.

"Of course, he told me about that later. After I calmed down about you being suspended." Ally and I laughed.

"I remember running with Ally to the shelter like dad told me to," I said, looking out the window again. "I wrote a letter to myself before I went into the experiment. It said that I was searching for you guys in the bunker when we first got there, but that I couldn't find you. And them telling me that you guys didn't make it to a bunker."

"Bunch of assholes," she muttered, and I nodded.

"More recently I was getting flashes of being in the military but couldn't find any record of it in the files they showed me," I continued. "That was part of what started me questioning it all and me and Ally looking into stuff. She found a file on me that said I was in the military for a few years before they put me into the experiment. Apparently, it said I had 'personal issues' so they put me in the experiment. After the dream I had, I thought it meant... I thought it meant that I had really killed Dad and it made me crazy or something. But it's such a relief to find out that didn't happen… Though it does make me curious what my 'personal issues' were."

"Maybe whatever they did to you was wearing off and you weren't as obedient anymore?" Ally said thoughtfully.

"That's a possibility," Mom said. "I've heard rumors of people defecting from some of the bunkers after they were able to fight whatever they were doing to them mentally."

"I don't know," I said. "Maybe. Maybe I'll find out when more of my memories come back."

"Either way," Ally said smiling at me. "It's all over now. That's not who you are. We all know that." I smiled back her, she had this way of making me feel better no matter what.

"I saw a sign for a small town up ahead," Mom said. "We should stop and see if we can salvage anything there. Hopefully there won't be any headhunters there…"

"Wait," I said leaning forward. "What do mean headhunters?" She sighed.

"Unfortunately, some of the people who survived, haven't been very…. civil about their living situations. Some people have turned to more… savage ways…"

"Meaning what?" Ally asked, though I wasn't sure I wanted to know.

"There's been stories about people in some smaller towns farther out that do not take kindly to visitors. They will kill anyone on sight and they… eat them…"

"Eat them?!" I shouted, shocked. "Like they eat humans??"

"Well apparently they don't *only* eat humans," she said, and I groaned. "But with most of the animals being killed off by the War, there's not a lot of food options around. So, they take advantage of their options, I guess. They're not everywhere from what I've heard, but we're bound to run into them at some point."

"I don't plan on being lunch," Ally said matter-of-factly.

"Agreed. I probably wouldn't taste very good anyway," Mom said trying to lighten the mood. "I've heard of other towns that are willing to trade, others still that are abandoned completely."

"Well I don't think we should just drive into town then," I said. "If there's headhunters there, it might get us killed. If there's people there, we might get swarmed for the car and everything. I think we should stop right outside town and see what we can see first."

"That sounds like a good plan," Ally said.

"Agreed," Mom said.

We stopped about a mile from this small town, I climbed out of the back seat and stretched. Ally and Mom got out and started digging through our bags of weapons.

"Next time I get the front," I said to Ally, and she laughed. "I'm too big for the back seat."

"You keep telling yourself that," she winked at me. Mom choked back a laugh and I laughed.

"You two are terrible," She said.

"We got it from you and Matt," Ally said, and Mom laughed. I reached into our bags and loaded up with weapons and an empty backpack for supplies we find in our trek into the town.

"You ready to go?" I asked and they both nodded. "I'll go first. Mom do you have any binoculars?"

"Unfortunately, no," she said. "Though it looks like it's surrounded by woods, so we should be good for cover." I looked toward the town and she was right, it was trees for as far as I could see. I looked up in the sky to find the sun. I knew it was about four in the afternoon. Though I wasn't sure how I knew that. Probably training in the military.

"Looks like we have a few hours till nightfall," I said. "Hopefully we can get in and out before then. Though if it's abandoned, we might stay here for the night."

"Let's go check it out and we'll go from there," Ally replied, obviously telling that I was worried. She reached up and gave me a kiss. I smiled and started walking in the direction of the town keeping my head on a swivel. I heard Ally and Mom fall into step behind me. I had a rifle in my hands, ready to go and defend us at any moment.

CHAPTER 13

We walk for about twenty minutes with nothing in sight other than the trees. A few times I would here a twig snap and would point my rifle, only to see a deer or rabbit wandering by us. I felt Ally's hand on my back each time, she could tell I was on edge. I would nod and continue on. Finally, after about 30 minutes of walking, I can see a few buildings through the trees. I slow down so that Ally and Mom can walk beside me and nod in that direction. They nod in response with guns in hand and we walk slowly toward the buildings. I'm breathing slowly so I can hear for anything ahead of us. So far, I only hear our own footsteps.

We reach the edge of the tree line and I stop, crouching down. Ally and Mom join me, both looking ahead of us at the buildings. They look old and worn down, some had their roofs caved in, others were missing siding. It looked like an old west small town, a ghost town. I couldn't see any movement or hear anything coming from the buildings. I leaned closer to Mom and Ally so they could hear me better.

"I think you guys should wait here, while I check it out," I whisper and surprisingly, both of them shot me a look.

"Or we could split up and all check it out faster," Mom whispered back, and I frowned. "We can take care of ourselves, Leo. I promise." She gestured to our weapons and I sighed.

"Fine," I said, knowing this wasn't the time or place to argue about it. I looked at the buildings closest to us. There were three closest to us, we were behind them, there were a few farther past them. "Mom you go towards that building on the left. Al you take the right one and I'll take the middle one. Don't go inside, just try and look in the windows and see if you can see anyone. I wanna see if there's anyone here before we search for supplies. We'll go around these ones before moving around the other ones. Then we'll go building by building just to be sure. Fair?" They both nod. "Let's go."

We slowly walk towards the buildings, and I don't like the idea of splitting up at all, even this close together. However, I knew they could both handle themselves, but it still made me worried. I glanced to my right and saw Ally with her rifle up looking towards her building. Mom on the left was the same. I smiled a little and did the same. Rifle on the ready, eyes switching between the windows on the building in front of me. I got to the building and crouched below the closest window. I slowly rose up to look inside. It looked like an old post office. I could see packages and envelopes laying around on the floor and the desk. I didn't see any people or movement. I crouch down again and move to the next window. More packages, looking like the back of the post office, I could see the post office totes on shelves. I moved around the right side of the building, toward the front. I lost sight of Ally and Mom, but I focused on what I was doing.

I didn't see anything ahead of me past the building. No movement, good sign. I reach the front of the building, walking along the front, looking in the windows and the door off its hinges. Still nothing. I glanced toward the right, Ally coming around the right side of her building, looking in windows, her rifle leading the way. Left, Mom doing the same. They both are satisfied that they didn't see anything, they head towards me in the middle.

We all head towards the buildings across the street. I gesture for Ally to go to the right one, she nods and walks that way. Mom automatically heads toward the left one. I focus on the one in front of me, it looks like a general store. Part of me is surprised that there are still small towns like this that would have a general store. But the other part realizes that farther from the big cities, people probably miss the small simple life.

I approach the front, the door missing completely, I look inside swinging my rifle from left to right, nothing. Lots of things cover the floor, I don't focus to much on these things, forcing myself to look for movement or people. I don't see anything; I move around the outside of the building to the left. Glancing around me and into windows as I pass them. I'm about to round the corner behind the building when I hear a scream to my left, Mom. I run towards the building on my left, rounding the side and almost run into my mom.

"Mom!" I say as Ally rounds the corner behind me, rifle raised. "Are you okay?"

"I'm sorry," she said, breathing heavily. I looked around her and saw a body of a man, who had obviously been dead for a while. He had part of his head missing, his skull empty, I saw animal claw marks all over his body. He had fingers missing on one of his hands and his entire left leg was gone below the knee. "I'm sorry, it just scared me. I'm sorry."

"It's okay, Mom," I said, peeling my eyes away from the body to look at her. I hear Ally walk away coughing, obviously not taking the sight very well. The smell was worse, but I focused on my mom. She was trying to steady her breathing, through her mouth, she had her nose covered from the smell. "It's okay. I'm sure it wasn't pleasant coming around and seeing that."

"I was just focused on ahead of me, then I saw it out of the corner of my eye and... it just scared me," she said, finally catching her breath. I look around us again, still not sure if we're alone. Ally is farther away from us, by the corner of the back of the building. She catches my eye and shows a weak smile. I'm surprised she didn't have a stronger stomach about this stuff being a nurse, but then I realize she probably didn't spend any time with dead bodies with this much decomposition. For some reason it doesn't bother me as much as I thought it would, but I'm sure the military training probably had something to do with that too.

"Come on," I said leading them towards the front of the building. "Let's start searching for supplies. I haven't seen any evidence of anyone here yet, so I think we're okay." She nods and Ally comes up next to us as we head around the front. I push open the door to what looks like an old diner, tables and booths around the room, with a bar on the left and stools in front of it. I lead into the room and automatically head toward the door behind the bar that leads to the kitchen. I'm immediately hit by the stench of death again. There are flies everywhere and I can see the body in the corner of the kitchen, worse off than the one outside. I swallow hard and look around the kitchen, searching for anything of use. I see a pantry door to the left and open it, empty. I glance around quickly, not wanting to spend too much time with decomp Bob in the corner. I see a kitchen knife on the table, I pick it up and head back into the dining room. Ally looks up at me in question and I hold up the knife.

"No food," I said. "Another decomp Bob in there, I'm thinking about calling the health department." She laughed. I smile, trying to break the tension.

"They'll have to shut down," Ally said simply. "It'll sure hurt profits." I laugh.

"Find anything out here?" I ask looking around. Ally pulls a shot gun out from under the counter and a box of shells.

"They had good security," She said lightly. I raise my eyebrows and smile.

"No kidding," I agreed. Mom walks around from the corner, which I'm assuming is where the rest rooms or back office is. She sets down a first aid kit on the table. "That'll come in handy." I pull off the backpack I'm wearing so we can load up the stuff we found here. After I put it back on, we head out the door and go to the general store next door.

We go through all the buildings in the small town, finding some canned food, bottled water, more weapons, and first aid supplies. My backpack is full by the time we reach the last building, a small motel by look of it. There are only six rooms, three upstairs, two downstairs and an office.

"We should stay here for the night," I say, pulling off my backpack and setting it on the bed in the last room upstairs. "I'll go get the car and bring it over so we can get going in the morning, first thing."

"I'll go with you," Ally said, and I looked at Mom.

"You guys are good," she said. "I'll take the room next door. Maybe they still have running water." I laugh and nod. I grab my rifle, leaving my backpack on the bed.

"Let's go Al," I say. "We'll be back soon Mom." She smiles and leads the way out of the room, she goes into the next room and we head down the stairs and back outside. The sun is starting to go down, we probably have another hour of daylight, if that.

We walk back towards the woods we entered from, keeping our eyes peeled for movement still. I know I want to park the car between the buildings and cover it with something before we turn in for the night, as to not draw attention to it if someone comes through the town.

"We're gonna be fine," Ally said taking my free hand, the other is on the trigger guard on the rifle across my chest. "Relax."

"I know," I said sighing. "I just wanna be sure." She laughed and I looked at her sideways. "What?"

"You were always kind of paranoid," she said lightly, not trying to be mean, just honest. "Now you seem more so, though, you seem calmer about it now. If that makes sense."

"I'm guessing it has to do with whatever they trained me for in the military," I mused. "I'm betting it was something like handling stress under pressure type thing." She nodded as we walked along the through the trees.

"Probably."

"I can tell the time just by looking at the sun," I started. "I don't remember being able to do that before."

"I don't remember you being able to do that either," she said. "Apparently, that training can come in handy." She laughed and I smiled a little. "What's going on in your head?"

"I don't know," I sighed, staring ahead for a few steps in silence. "It just bothers me that I can't remember everything yet. I have all this training apparently, but I don't even remember having it. Hell, even Mom back there-" gesturing behind us, back to the town "-I know she's my mother. I recognize her, but I don't remember the feelings associated with her. Other than these flashes here and there. It's just... frustrating." She squeezed my hand and stopped me, turning me towards her.

"I understand," she said lightly, reaching up and caressing my face. I lean my face into her hand enjoying its warmth and her touch. "I've been there, baby. It takes time for it all to come back. I know it sucks; I know it's frustrating. But I'm gonna be here every step of the way helping you figure it all out. I've known you almost all my life, I probably know you better than you know yourself, even when you had your memory." I smiled and she chuckled. I leaned down and kissed her.

"I love you," I whispered softly, pushing my forehead against hers and closing my eyes for a moment. "And I'm sorry." She leaned back and kissed my forehead.

"I love you," she whispered back. "And don't apologize. You're stuck with me." I sighed and breathed in her scent, trying to relax a bit. I opened my eyes and turned to continue walking. I didn't want to be out here after dark.

We got to the car and drove it back on the road we were on earlier. It only took a few minutes to make it back to town driving. I parked the car between the motel and the postal office. I moved anything we didn't need inside to the trunk, so it won't be easily seen if someone found the car. I had found a tarp earlier that was torn slightly, but we cover the car with it anyway. Better safe than sorry. We walked back into the motel and found Mom in the main lobby area stoking a fire in the fireplace. We had brought a couple pots we found from the general store earlier. Ally and I sat down on the moth-eaten sofa in front of the fire and watched Mom work on opening canned food.

"Any problems?" She asked, dumping what looked like pork and beans into the pot over the fire.

"Nope," Ally replied leaning against me, with my arm across her shoulders. My mom smiled and I cocked my head to the side, questioningly.

"Nothing," she said shaking her head. "I'm just so glad we're all together. I'm so proud of you both. You've grown more than I could ever imagine." I smiled and Ally sniffled beside me, I squeezed her shoulder into me. "I love you both so much."

"I love you, too, Mom," Ally said, and Mom smiled, tears in her eyes.

"Me too," I said, and Mom laughed.

"Just like your father," she said. "He used to say that all the time." I felt a pang in my heart, knowing that I still don't remember that, a frown on my face. Mom didn't notice, she was back focused on the food and the fire. Ally however did, she glanced up at me and squeezed my thigh. I smiled down at her and kissed her forehead.

"Dinner is almost ready," Mom said, stirring with a spoon. She had a few random bowls next to her. "It's not much, but it'll do."

"It's five-star quality, Mom," I said, and she laughed, as she dished up our bowls and handed them over.

We ate mostly quiet. Just enjoying the food. A funny comment here or there, but mostly a comfortable silence. It was nice, given that we were in a post-apocalyptic world and we were on our own, me with incomplete memory, my Ally with her loving attitude and my mother with her fierce loyalty to us both. It was like a dream, an odd one, but a dream none the less.

"Well I think it's time for bed," Mom said standing up after letting the fire die out.

"I'm going to stay up to keep watch," I said matter-of-factly. Both of them began their protests.

"We already searched the town, Leo," Ally said. "We're fine. We'll hear anyone before they get upstairs to us."

"We all need rest, honey," Mom said. "We'll be fine." I sighed and stood up, holding up my hands.

"You two are impossible for a knight in shining armor," I said joking.

"More like tin foil," Ally smirked. Mom laughed.

"Geez, woman," I countered. "You like to kill any chivalry I have, don't you?" She smiled.

"I'd rather have a partner than a knight anyway," she said, and I sighed.

"I'm going to bed," Mom cut in. "You two can stay up and argue." She smiled and kissed us both on the cheek before heading towards the stairs.

"Night, Mom," I call after her and I look at Ally. "Ready for bed?"

"Yes," she said stiffly a yawn, taking my hand and leading me towards the stairs.

I shut the door to our room and kick my shoes off. Ally does the same and climbs into the bed, which is dusty, but it works. I lean my rifle against the bed and put a pistol under my pillow. I glance out the window for a minute and Ally groans.

"Come on babe," she said patting the dusty bed beside her. "We need sleep. We've had a long day." I smile and climb in beside her. She lays her head on my chest and I wrap my arm around her.

"I'm glad we got out of that bunker and found Mom and all," I start. "But I can't help but think about all those we left behind."

"I know," she said softly. "I was thinking about that too. But maybe if we get some place safer with more people, maybe we can find a way to fight back, to free everyone."

"Unfortunately, I don't think we're gonna find enough people to go up against them," I said sadly. "They have an army. They have the weapons to withstand anyone. I think the only way we could do anything would be to have someone on the inside to take down the security from the inside…" She leaned back to look at me, I could barely make out her face in the darkness.

"Is that what you're wanting to do?" she asked, again never judging, just curious.

"I don't know," I said honestly. "I want to save them, or at least try to give them a chance. But I know we couldn't do it alone; we would need help. We have to save ourselves before we can save anyone else. I can't go charging in there doing something stupid just to be heroic." She chuckled.

"Good," she said rubbing her hand over my chest. "I can't lose you again."

"And I can't lose you," I whisper softly and kissed her forehead.

"Mmmm," she smiled and snuggled in closer to me, putting her leg over mine. I squeezed her closer to me. "I love you."

"I love you gorgeous. Sleep tight."

* * *

I'm back on the other side of the fence moving bodies away from it. Where I saw my dad, dying by my hand. I stood up shocked, staring at the man who looked like my dad. I looked down at my hands, my body, covered in blood. My hands started shaking as I looked back and forth between the man, dead now, and my own blood covered body. He hadn't said my name, I realized, but seeing him, looking like my father triggered something in my brain. I remembered my father. They had messed with my brain before they brought me top side for training. I hadn't remembered anything from before, not even my name, they had told me my name.

That was a little over two years ago by this point, but I remembered my father. I slowly backed away from the pile of bodies, the man who looked like my father, the blood. I was trembling from head to toe and was shaking my head.

"No, no, no, no," I muttered to myself as I backed away. The other soldiers around me took notice of this and stopped moving bodies to look at me.

"Parks," the closest one said, he was above me in rank, but I don't know his name. "What's the matter with you?"

"No, no, no, no," I muttered still backing away. "I can't do this. I can't. I remember my father. I can't do this. This isn't right." The soldier raised his eyebrows, catching on to what was happening.

"Wilson," he shouted at the other soldier who was still moving bodies. He stood and looked at the superior officer. "Take Parks back to the bunker. Get him to the doctor. They're gonna have to wipe him again."

"Yes, sir," he said and grabbed my arm, steering me away from the bodies, back toward the gate in the fence. I let him lead me back inside the fence and to the main building. We went inside and he took me into what looked like a lab. A doctor was there, at least I'm assuming he was a doctor, given his white lab coat.

"What is it? Is he injured?" He asked the soldier still holding my arm, while looking at me still covered in blood.

"The Major told me to bring him to you," Wilson said. "Said you would have to wipe him again." The doctor sighed, and pinched the bridge of his nose.

"That's the third one this month," he said. "What happened? What did he remember?"

"I'm not sure," he replied They were talking like I wasn't there. "He was helping us move bodies and then he just stopped and started muttering about how he couldn't do it. He said he remembered his father." The doctor nodded and sighed again.

"Okay, okay," he said stepping forward and taking my other arm. The soldier released me. "I'll take him. We'll have to wipe him and put him into the program downstairs. Thank you soldier."

The soldier nodded and left. The doctor steered me into a room from this one and told me to sit on the bed, I did, still shaking. A nurse came into the room and laid me down.

"Another one?" she asked the doctor.

"Yes, apparently," he replied, messing with vials and syringes beside the bed. "I really thought we had got the formula right after the last one. But apparently not. We'll just have to keep trying." He stuck something into my arm and I fell asleep.

CHAPTER 14

I felt a hand go over my mouth and another hand shake my shoulder to wake me up. My eyes shot open, already reaching for my gun under my pillow. I calmed when I realized it was Ally. She had her hand over my mouth but released it when she saw that I was awake. She put a finger to her lips and pointed to her ear and then the door. I figured out what she meant when I listened, and I heard noises coming from downstairs. I grabbed the gun from under my pillow and slowly stood up from the bed. Ally was beside me already with a pistol in her hand. I gestured for her to stay behind me and she nodded.
I walked slowly to the door, trying to not make much noise. I turned the handle slowly and pulled the door open. The noises got louder. It sounded like someone was banging around pots downstairs. I stepped out of our room and immediately saw my mom coming out of her room. I put a finger to my lips and she nodded as I slowly walked to the stairs. It was early and the sun was barely coming up outside, so I looked down the stairs first, but couldn't see any movement. I took the first couple of steps down but stopped on the third when it squeaked. I froze when the noises downstairs stopped. They resumed a couple of sec-

onds later, so I continued down the stairs.

I reached the bottom and followed the noises into the main lobby where we had had dinner the night before. I could feel Ally and my mother behind me. As soon as I entered the room I discovered what was making the noises. I lowered my gun immediately when I saw the dog that was licking our dinner pot from the night before. I chuckled and turned to Ally and Mom.

"It's just a dog," I said, and they sighed, relieved. "He's just hungry by the looks of it." I walked a little farther into the room and the dog stopped licking the pot to look at me. He was a bigger dog, black with a little white on his chest from what I could see. He looked scared mostly, but cautious of me. I put my gun in the back of my pants again and showed him my hands. He still didn't move, just tilted his head a little. He was cute and obviously under fed. He was skin and bones.

"Hey, buddy," I said softly, walking slowly towards him. "It's okay. I'm not gonna hurt you." I got within a couple feet of him and heard him start to growl a little. I stopped walking and knelt on the floor with my hands out to him so he could come to me. He stopped growling and sniffed the air a little, obviously unsure of what to do. I felt Ally come up beside me, kneeling as well. She had one of bowls from last night in her hand.

"You want some more?" she asked softly, and he stood up. We could tell he was hungry, but still concerned about us. He took a step towards us, then another. He came right up to Ally and automatically started licking the bowl she held. She reached out and pet his head and he paused his licking for a second, but then continued, deciding that there was no threat compared to the food. "Good boy, you're just hungry huh?"

"He's cute," Mom said from behind us, leaning against the wall by the stairs. "Might be good to keep him around to have another set of ears and eyes for us." I reached out and pet him as well, he was soft, but I could feel his ribs through his fur.

"I agree," I said. "Will you grab another can of food, please? He's super malnourished." She walked away and brought another can of pork and beans. He looked up as soon as she opened it, head titled to the side. I smiled. "We won't hurt you, buddy. It's okay." Mom dumped the whole can into the bowl he was already licking, and he ate it all quickly. I opened a bottle of water and poured into the bowl when he was done. He drank it happily with his tail wagging.

When he was done, he went straight up to Ally and licked her face. We all laughed and petted him.

"I'm surprised there's any dogs left to be honest," Mom said, sitting on the couch next to us. "Though I'm sure the ones who survived the War just became feral and lived on."

"Probably," Ally agreed. "What are we gonna call him? Wait it is a him, right?" She lifted his back leg a little. "Yep, it's a him." We all laughed.

"I'm thinking Butch," I said, and Ally scoffed. "What?" Shooting her a defensive look.

"Such a guy," she said rolling her eyes at me. She rubbed the dog's ears and he leaned into her. Mom laughed.

"Well what do you wanna call him then?" I countered.

"I'm thinking Duke," she said, and his ears perked up. "Oh, you like that one huh? Duke?" His tail thumped on the floor.

"Duke it is," Mom said.

"Apparently so," I agreed and stood up. I looked out the window the sun was fully up now. "We should get some breakfast and get going."

We all got up and got ready to start the day and Duke following Ally around everywhere she went. After breakfast, we loaded in the car, Mom driving, me in front and Ally in the back with Duke. He laid down after about 30 minutes on the road with his head in her lap.

"I think I've been replaced," I said jokingly. Duke looked up at me before resting back on her lap.

"I mean he is pretty cute," Ally said, and his tail thumped again. Mom laughed as I mocked hurt.

"You're both so mean to me," I said.

"You're a big boy," Mom said lightly. "You'll be fine." Ally laughed. I looked back at Duke, who picked his head up and looked back at me.

"Come on dude," I said to him. "Us guys are supposed to stick together." Duke thumped his tail a couple times, sighed, and put his head back in Ally's lap. We all laughed. "Even the dog has taken sides. Damn."

"Love you baby," Ally said grinning. I rolled my eyes but smiled at her.

"Oh, I had another dream again," I said, facing forward again. I explained it all to them, given it was right after the whole thinking I killed my dad.

"Oh wow," Ally said. "So it was that the stuff wasn't working anymore."

"Apparently," I said, still playing through it in my head. Ally reached up and grabbed my shoulder, squeezing it.

"It's okay, babe," she said. I grabbed her hand and squeezed it back, kissing her palm.

"I wonder how many more there are," Mom mused. "Ones that got out when their memories started coming back."

"I don't know," I said.

We drove on for a few hours. Stopping here and there at random gas stations that were abandoned. We were able to get some fuel at a couple of them. We even put some in gas cans we found, just in case. We kept driving till around noon, and stopped for lunch, stretching our legs. Mom pulled out her map on the trunk of the car and was looking at the signs around the truck stop we were stopped at. I was eating and leaned against the car next to mom.

Ally was a little further away throwing a stick for Duke. He was good at fetch and was having fun. I loved watching her play with him. She was laughing and having a good time. I smiled and then focused my attention back on Mom and her map.

"How we looking?" I asked. She had drawn a line from where we started to just outside what was San Francisco, California to where we were now.

"We're about two hours from Portland," she said, pointing to it in Oregon. "I'd like to make it at least to Seattle before we stop for the night again. Or at least outside of Seattle, maybe on the other side. I don't like the idea of stopping in a big city for the night."

"Me neither."

"We're gonna have to drive through it if wanna make good time," she said thoughtfully. "Granted going around would be safer, but it would take longer. Same with Portland, for that matter. Once we get into Canada tomorrow we should be fine in terms of other people. They were already pretty sparse before the war. Though, supplies might be harder to come by, so it might a good idea to stop in either Seattle or Portland to stock up. What do you think?" I was studying the map beside her.

"I'd rather avoid the big cities if possible," I said. "But I agree, we're gonna have to stock up to get through Canada. How much fuel do we have right now?"

"We've got a full tank, so 13 gallons there," she said opening the trunk to look. "Another 10 gallons in gas cans." She closed the trunk again.

"I think we should go around Portland and Seattle and stock up in Vancouver, here," I said point to it, just on the other side of the Canadian border. "They always Canadians were nicer than Americans, right?" She laughed.

"I'm not sure if that still applies nowadays," she said, Ally and Duke had walked over by this point. She wrapped her arm around my waist and kissed me. Duke laid down at her feet panting with a stick in his mouth.

"Hey babe," she said, then looked down at the map with us. "What we doing?"

"Trying to decide where to stock up to make it through Canada," Mom said simply. "Because, unfortunately, Canada is a little spread out when it comes to stops like this. Leo thinks we should go around Portland and Seattle and stock up in Vancouver. How about you?" Ally leaned over the map.

"It doesn't look like there's many roads to go around them without going completely in the other direction, but then we would have to cut back to hit Vancouver," She said pointing to the major roads in Washington. "If we're wanting to avoid some of the bigger cities I think we should stock up in Portland and then cut over here. It'll allow us to miss Seattle and Vancouver completely and will only add a couple hours on to our trip." I followed her finger as she pointed along. She was right, especially, if Seattle was bombed during the War. Portland was smaller, so hopefully not as affected. I nodded slowly.

"That could work," I said. "Mom?"

"Works for me," she said, marking it on the map. "Seattle was probably wiped off the map during the War anyway."

"That's what I was thinking," Ally said. "Portland was smaller, so hopefully wasn't a target." I smirked at her loving how much we were on the same wavelength.

"Then it's settled," Mom said, folding up her map again. "We'll stock up in Portland and then find a smaller town past it to put up for the night, hopefully."

We all piled back in the car, me driving this time and Mom in the back with Duke and Ally beside me. She had her hand on my thigh while I was driving. Mom had fallen asleep with Duke sleeping with his head in her lap.

"What was that smirk for earlier?" Ally asked me softly, as to not wake Mom. I smiled and squeezed her hand on my thigh.

"I just love how you practically read my mind," I said. "I had just thought about Portland being smaller and not a target right before you said it." She chuckled softly and squeezed my hand back.

"We always used to do that," she said. "I would think something and you would say it or vice versa. It came in handy when we wanted to have silent conversations in front of people. We were always pretty good at reading each other, our facial expressions, our tones, everything, and I think it drove your parents nuts sometimes." We both laughed. "We would be totally silently looking at each other across the dinner table with them and then we would both just start laughing. They were always so confused, but they found it cute."

"I can't wait to be able to remember all of it for myself," I said sadly. "Don't get me wrong, I love you telling me all this. It's just not the same, you know?" She nodded and squeezed my hand again.

"I know," she said. "You will. It'll all come back eventually. I promise."

"You should get some sleep, baby," I said, and she nodded.

"Wake me up if you need me," she said, leaving her hand on my thigh and leaning her head back and shutting her eyes.

I drove on for a while, Ally, Mom, and Duke all asleep. I liked driving, granted I did in the experiment and obviously I still did. I let my mind wander.

* * *

I was in a car, behind the wheel, I was younger. Probably 16 or so. I looked over and my dad was in the passenger seat. We were sitting in the driveway of our house.

"Always make sure you check your mirrors," he said. "You wanna make sure they're in the right position before you go anywhere. You don't want to have to be adjusting them when you need them." I nodded and looked in the rearview mirror adjusting it so I could see completely out the back window while sitting comfortably. "Your side mirrors you wanna adjust so you can just see the side of the car, it'll help you when you're driving to stay in your lane and when backing up and what not." I did as I was told, adjusting the side mirrors.

"Ok," I said.

"Mirrors all good?" He asked and I nodded. "Okay, put your foot on the brake and put the car in reverse." I did. "Now when you're backing out you wanna make sure you're watching your mirrors, but also looking around you, because mirrors can't show you everything. Slowly ease off the brake till you start moving."

I let off the brake a little too much and then slammed it back down when we moved too quickly, and Dad laughed.

"It's okay son," he said. "You have to get a feel for the car. Each car you drive will be a little different. You have to get used to how touchy the brakes are and the gas pedal. You'll get used to it. Try it again." I let go of the brake a little slower this time and we rolled backwards. "Be sure you're checking your mirrors to make sure you don't go in the grass, and around you to make sure there's no other cars around." I checked my mirrors and kept the wheel steady. Looked around behind us and the street was clear.

"Now when you reach the end of the driveway," he continued. "You're gonna turn the wheel in the same way you want the back of the car to go. Make sure you don't turn too quickly. You could take out the mailbox and your mom will be pissed." I laughed and did as he said. I made it out of the driveway and stepped on the brake again to stop the car. "Now hold the brake and put the car in drive. Then you're going to slowly let off the brake and slowly step on the gas a little. Same thing as the brake, you have to get a feel for it. We aren't going drag racing." I laughed again and did as I was told. We moved forward and dad continued to talk me through everything.

* * *

Ally twitched beside me in her sleep, pulling me from my memory. Her hand was still on my thigh and I put my hand over hers and she settled again. I smiled at the memory of my dad teaching me how to drive. I was glad to have another memory of him, especially one of just us. He was amazing and I felt another hint of sadness that I won't ever see him again. I know that there are still memories I have of him that will come back. I look forward to getting them back. I glanced in the rearview mirror and saw that Mom was awake.

"You okay?" she asked softly, making sure not to wake Ally.

"Yeah," I said smiling. "I just had a flashback of Dad teaching me how to drive." I saw her smile.

"That was one thing you two bonded over a lot," she said. "He wanted to teach you everything he could about cars. He always said that that's what his father and him bonded over, so he wanted that with you." I cocked my head a little at the mention of my grandfather.

"Did I know him?" I asked.

"He died before you were born unfortunately," she said sadly. "I had only met him a few times before that, when your father and I were dating."

"How old was he when his dad died?"

"He was about your age now actually," she said thoughtfully, looking out the window. "His father smoked a lot, he got cancer. It was rough on Matt; he was close to his father. His mother had died when he was little, so Leo was all he had."

"Leo?" I was surprised and she chuckled.

"Leonardo," she said. "Yes, you were named after him. Though I fought for just Leo. Leonardo was such an old-fashioned name." I laughed a little. "Mathew obviously after your father." I nodded. So, I was named after my grandfather and my father, I felt a swell of pride in my chest. "Your grandfather was a good man. He would be proud of you, too. He always joked about Matt and I getting married even when we first started dating. He said he expected us to have at least five kids. I told him he was crazy." I laughed again.

"How did you two meet?" I asked, feeling bad. I probably had already heard the story before, but couldn't remember it.

"In high school," she mused. "At the end of senior year he had asked me to prom, and it took off from there. We were so close back then; you and Ally remind me of us." I smiled at that and glanced over at Ally, still sleeping. "We dated for a few years and then he asked me to marry him. Shortly before his dad died, actually. We got married about a year after that, but we didn't want to have kids yet. We were both still in college and we wanted to make sure that when we had kids we could give them a great life. We waited till after we graduated and got decent jobs. We moved into that house and then two months later I was pregnant with you."

"Of course, I always wanted a girl," she said and smiled at me in the mirror. "Don't get me wrong you were my little boy through and through." I laughed. "I had just always wanted a girl. We tried again after a year or so. Then came Mandy…" She trailed off.

"You must miss her," I said, feeling a pang again.

"I do, every day. But she was in so much pain by the end," she whispered softly, staring out the window again, not really seeing anything, just in her head. "It was better that way; she went to a better place. Especially after all this. It was rough for your father and I after that."

"In my letter to myself," I started. "I mentioned that you and Dad fought a lot and that I would focus on school to escape. Though when I was told that you both had died, I was glad you went together, because even after Mandy died you still had each other." I heard her sniffle and I saw her wipe her eyes.

"Yes," she said, I could hear the pain in her voice, but she continued. "We fought a lot after she died, but you're right, we had each other and you of course. You were still young, and it was hard to deal with for a while. There were days where I couldn't get out of bed and your father would take care of you. He would always come check on me though. He was supportive of course, but he was in pain too. We went to counseling and worked through it. By the time you were older, we were better. We knew that even though we had lost Mandy, we still had you and we had to take care of you."

"I'm sorry for bringing all this up again, Mom," I said. "I'm sure I've heard it all before, I just don't remember…" She reached up and squeezed my shoulder.

"It's okay sweetie," she said softly. "It's just been a long time since I talked about it all. Old feelings and all that. But we got through all that, and we'll get through this too." I smiled at her in the mirror.

CHAPTER 15

"Looks like we're about ten minutes from Portland," Ally said beside me, making me jump. She squeezed my hand letting me know she was letting me and Mom have our time. I squeezed back; she was truly amazing.

"Yep," Mom said leaning forward. "I'm thinking we try to stick to the outskirts of the city. As much as we need to stock up, I'd rather not go directly through the city."

"Agreed," I said. "Food and fuel are our top priorities. I think we're good on weapons for now, but if we can get some of those too, great. Hell, if we can find one of those super center stores still open, we'll be set." They both laughed.

"Somehow I don't think they will be," Ally said, and I laughed.

"Well, a guy can hope," I joked.

We drove the rest of the way into Portland in silence. All of us watching out the window looking for people or places that looked good for supplies. Even Duke was sitting up looking outside with us. I got off the main road when I could see skyscrapers in the distance, wanting to stay out of the middle of the city. As soon as I got off the main road though, I started seeing people everywhere. All looking malnourished and weak, but they watched us as we passed. It made me uneasy. I didn't want to have to fight our way through these people.

"Looks like there's a truck stop up there," Ally said pointing to an old gas sign ahead of us. I nodded and heading towards it. We pulled into the parking lot and saw people standing outside. They all turned when we pulled in. Some of them had weapons, but they weren't pointing any at us, yet at least.

"I don't like this," I said as I parked by a gas pump.

"Relax," Mom said. "We'll play nice first, but we don't want to come off too confrontational. They don't look like headhunters." I put my pistol in the back of my pants before nodding and opening my door.

We climbed out of the car, Duke jumping out with us, and sticking close to Ally. I liked that he was protective of her and he could keep her safe when I couldn't. Mom headed over to the people, waving at them as she approached. Ally, Duke, and I stayed back closer to the car. Mom had the most experience with this kind of stuff, so I was fine letting her take the lead. I could see them talking for a bit, nodding towards us and the car. I couldn't hear what they were saying, but body language didn't seem threatening so far. Mom headed back towards us and we waited for her to get back to us. I kept my eyes on the people behind her as she walked.

"They said there's fuel here," she said when she got to us. "And they're willing to trade for it. They said we could have 20 gallons for some weapons and ammo." I glanced at Ally but nodded.

"I'm okay with that," I said. "We're at about a half tank now. So, five in the tank and 15 in the trunk with the 10 we already have. What are we gonna give them though?"

"One of the shotguns and some shells," Ally said automatically. "We have what three or four of them? We still have the rifles from the bunker and I think we should keep those. Hell, if they have food too, we can give them two of the shotguns."

"I'm thinking just one," Mom said. "We don't know what else we will run into and we can trade another one of them for. They don't have any food that they're willing to trade, just the gas."

"Okay," I said, opening the trunk. I kept my body in between the trunk and the people we're dealing with, to make sure they couldn't see all that we had. I grab one of the shotguns and three boxes of shells, leaving us with three shotguns and about ten more boxes of shells. "Do they have any gas cans we could have? We only have one left empty."

"I'm not sure," Mom said. "Grab another box of shells and we'll offer it if they do." I grab what she says and close the trunk. I walk back over with Mom towards the men after making sure that Duke would stay with Ally. He sat at her feet as we walked away.

"We have a shotgun and three boxes of shells," Mom told them as we approached them. "Four boxes if we can get a gas can or two from you." The men look at each other for a minute and then look at the stuff in my hands. The one man nods and the shorter one heads inside the building. He comes back out with two gas cans and sets them down on the ground in front of us. I hand him the shotgun and shells and pick up the cans.

"The pumps on," the one man said, obviously in charge. "Already set to a 20-gallon limit."

"Thank you, gentlemen," Mom said and bowed her head a little to the man in charge. "Pleasure doing business with you." I nod at them and they both nod back, and I turn and follow Mom back to the car.

I fill up the car first and then the three gas cans we have. After moving some stuff around in the trunk, I get everything loaded up and get back in the driver's seat.

"See that wasn't so bad," Ally said squeezing my leg as I pull out of the parking lot. I laughed and Mom chuckled.

"Most people out here are just trying to survive," she said. "And most of them are willing to trade for stuff they need. We just have to be friendly and not overly confrontational."

"Yes, mother," I said sarcastically. Ally slapped my leg and Mom laughed.

"Thank you, Ally," she said, and Ally grinned at her. I laughed.

We drove through the outskirts of Portland still looking for more places we could get stuff. Some places already had signs in front of the that read 'No Trades' or 'No Trespassing.' We avoided those places. We found one place that looked like an old grocery store. There wasn't a sign out front, but they looked heavily armed. Plenty of guys outside with guns, but surprisingly enough, there were women sitting by the main door who looked friendly enough. Mom told me to stop, so we pulled in. We went through the same routine, Mom approached them first, Ally, Duke, and I stayed by the car. She came back and said they have canned food to trade. I got out another shotgun and three boxes of shells. Ally put her hand on my chest to stop me.

"Maybe I should handle this one," she said lightly, taking the stuff out of my hands. I wanted to protest, but I didn't because of the look on her face. I trusted her and Mom to handle themselves. Plus, I knew she had a pistol in her jeans, same as me. "Duke will keep us safe. I promise."

"Okay," I said, and she kissed me before following Mom back towards the store. Duke following closely along beside her. They stopped for a moment to speak with the women at the entrance, gave them the shotgun and shells, and then followed them inside. I leaned against the car with my arms folded across my chest. I watched the men pacing in front of the store with their eyes on me as well. It made me nervous to not have them in my sight, but I knew they knew what they were doing.

About ten minutes later, they came out after the women with a few bags in each of their hands. They spoke with them for a few more minutes before heading back towards me. They put their bags in the trunk with the rest of our stuff and we all climbed back in the car.

"You okay?" I asked as soon as I shut my door.

"We're good, babe," Ally said softly, patting my leg as we pulled out of the parking lot. "We got about four- or five-days' worth of food and bottled water. They were nice. You just look a little intimidating. I figured it would better for us girls to handle it." She grinned at me and I laughed.

"Yes, ma'am," I said mockingly, and she slapped my thigh, Mom laughed.

"What time is it?" Ally asked and I looked up in the sky for the sun.

"About 4 or 5," I said. "We need to get out of the city and find a place for the night, preferably before dark."

"Agreed."

We drove for another hour or so, out past the city until we couldn't see the skyscrapers in the mirror anymore. I saw a sign for a bed and breakfast a couple miles ahead and we agreed that we would check it out if it was isolated. We pulled off the main road and kept following the signs. It was tucked away in the mountains, definitely isolated. We didn't see any movement outside, or inside from what we could see. We got out and I grabbed my rifle and led the way towards the house Ally and Mom behind me. Duke stayed close to me this time, sniffing around and looking with me. When we reached the front door, I was surprised that it was still attached. I opened it slowly and Duke darted inside. I followed slowly, sweeping my rifle from side to side.

We searched the whole house, room by room, it was empty, abandoned. We went back into the sitting room on the main floor and sat on the couch, Mom in the armchair, and Duke on the floor at Ally's feet. We ate some dinner, they still had running water, so we got to take a shower, granted a cold shower, but a shower none the less. It was just starting to get dark, so we called it a night, Ally, Duke, and I in one room up stairs and Mom in the room next to us. Duke laid down at the foot of the bed and I wrapped my arms around Ally. Falling asleep pretty easily.

* * *

I'm standing in a hospital room, I'm young, six or so. I can tell because I can only just barely see over the side of the hospital bed. Mandy is laying in it looking small and frail. My mom is sitting in the chair opposite me, on the other side of the bed. She's crying and holding Mandy's tiny hand. My dad is standing behind me his hands on my shoulders, and I can hear him crying too.

"Mommy," Mandy said. "I'm scared." I felt tears down my own face as I saw the fear in Mandy's eyes. My mom sniffled and wiped away some of her tears, scooting closer to Mandy.

"It's okay sweetie," she said softly, fighting back the tears. Trying to be strong for her daughter. "You've been so strong, so brave. You're my brave little girl. I love you so much. It's gonna be okay. You're gonna go to a safe place for a while, until we can be with you again, okay? We'll be with you again, I promise." She held Mandy's hand tightly in both her hands and smiled at her, kissing her hand. I reached out and took Mandy's other hand, she looked over at me.

"I love you, Manda-panda," I said softly, through my own tears. I was young and didn't fully understand what was happening, but I knew she was dying. She smiled at me and closed her eyes. I heard the heart monitor beep a few more times before it beeped loudly and continuously, flat lining. A nurse I hadn't noticed in the corner reached over and turned it off. My mom broke down in sobs. Laying her head on the bed next to her daughter. My father's hands shook on my shoulders and I could hear him crying. I cried harder as Mandy's hand fell from mine. I leaned over and hugged her hard.

My dad pulled me back and picked me up, carrying from the room with my mother still sobbing beside Mandy. He brought me out into the hallway kneeling down in front of me, setting me on my feet. He hugged me hard.

"It's okay, buddy," he said softly in my ear. "It's okay. She's in a better place now." He was still crying himself. "We'll see her again. We'll all be happy together in the better place." I didn't understand what this better place was, or why we couldn't go there now. I didn't ask. I just cried in my fathers' arms in the hallway, still hearing my mother crying in the room.

* * *

Duke's growl woke me, and I automatically grabbed my pistol from under my pillow. I sat up and looked at him. The sun wasn't up yet, but it was close, so I could see a little bit. He was at the door, hair raised on his back and lips raise to bare his teeth. I hopped out of the bed with Ally getting up beside me. I realized I had tears on my face and quickly wiped them away and walked toward the door. I listened but couldn't hear anything. I reached over and opened the door and Duke bolted out of the room and down the stairs. I followed quickly and quietly; pistol raised in front of me. He was at the front door, still growling, I opened that one as well. He bolted out the door towards where the car was parked. I heard yelling and could make out shapes around our car. Duke charged at them, they screamed and turned to run. There were two of them and they obviously weren't armed, otherwise they would have probably fired at him. I decided to save my bullets since they were already out of sight. Duke nipping at their heels as they went. I walked outside to the car, keeping my eyes on where the disappeared. I checked the doors, still locked. I opened the trunk, everything accounted for. Ally was standing at the door, watching me.

"We okay?" she asked as Mom appeared behind her.

"Looks like it," I said. "I don't see anything missing. Duke chased them off. I didn't hear any shots so I'm assuming they weren't armed."

"Is he gonna be okay?" Mom asked. I turned back towards where they disappeared and whistled loudly. We waited, and a few minutes later Duke came bounding back through the trees, tongue hanging out the side of his mouth.

"Who's a good boy?" Ally said as he went directly to her, she dropped to her knees and rubbed him behind his ears. He was panting heavily but wagging his tail. "Who's a good boy? You chased those guys off all on your own? Good boy!" He was loving it, licking at her face in between pants. I chuckled and closed the trunk again locking it. Headed back into the house with them.

"Well now that we're all awake," I said, sitting on the couch. "How about breakfast?" Ally laughed, sitting on the floor, leaning against my legs. Duke laid out next to her, still panting.

"I'll get some water for him," Mom said and disappeared into the kitchen that we had searched last night. Ally nudged my leg and I looked at her.

"You okay?" she asked.

"I had another memory come back," I said slowly, she cocked her head. "The day that Mandy died in the hospital…" A shadow crossed her face and I assumed that she already knew about that day from me telling her before. I felt more tears coming up from thinking about it and I sniffled, rubbing my nose. Ally stood and sat down across my lap, wrapping her arms around my neck. I buried my face in her shoulder and held her, letting some of the tears fall. I didn't care, I didn't feel embarrassed with her about crying or anything. She ran her hand through my hair and held me close and tightly.

"I'm sorry, baby," she said softly against my ear. "It's okay. It's okay. I'm here. It's okay." I shook from my tears and I faintly heard Mom come back in the room and Duke get up off the floor, heading towards her. I ignored it all, just me and Ally. I squeezed her so tightly I thought I would break her. She just ran her hand through my hair and squeezed me back until I couldn't cry anymore.

I loosened my grip on her and pulled my head back from her

shoulder, leaning my forehead against hers. She reached up and wiped my tears from my face. I couldn't help but laugh and she tilted her head.

"Just me crying," I said. "I don't seem very sexy or manly crying." She gently kissed me and leaned her forehead against mine again.

"You are the manliest man I've ever met," she said softly. "Crying doesn't make you weak, honey. Crying means you're strong enough to be vulnerable. That makes you more manly than anyone, and way sexier than ever." She grinned and I chuckled.

"What did I do to deserve you?" I whispered softly, taking her face in both my hands, pulling it away from mine. I looked deep into her emerald eyes and I swear I could see my future with her.

"You loved me when I was unlovable," she said softly, tears in her own eyes. She blinked and one fell, I wiped it away with my thumb. I traced her lips with my other thumb.

"You were always lovable," I replied. "You just needed someone to show you that you were." She smiled and more tears fell, she pulled me close and kissed me hard. Nothing sexual, just pure passion and love. I kissed her back just as hard, pouring as much love and passion as she gave me into it. She pulled back and rested her forehead against mine again, eyes closed. We sat there for a few silent minutes, just breathing together. I heard Mom enter the room again and clear her throat.

"I made breakfast," she said, and Ally pulled back from me, wiping my face and then her own. "If you're up for it."

"Sorry, Mom," I said, standing after Ally. "I had a little breakdown there. Just more memories." I laughed it off.

"It's okay sweetheart," Mom said as we followed her into the kitchen. "We're all allowed break downs every once in a while. It's what makes us human." She smiled softly at me as we sat around the little table in the kitchen. I smiled back and noticed Duke on the floor already eating his breakfast.

We ate quietly. My mind still processing everything from my memory to my moment with Ally. I will marry her; I know that now. Even without all my memories, even without everything. I will marry her and live the rest of my life with her. She is the one who completes me, there's no doubt in my mind. I would die for her. I would kill for her. I would do anything in my power for her.

"We should head out after breakfast," Mom said, pulling me from my thoughts.

"Agreed," I said lightly. We finished eating and packed all our stuff up then loaded everything in the car. Ally driving this time, me in the front, Mom, and Duke in the back. We headed out and went north heading toward the Canadian border. I briefly wonder if it'll be hard to cross the border. Though I doubt it, they're probably in the same boat we're in here.

We keep heading north finally crossing into Canada with no problems. We stop at an abandoned gas station for lunch and get some gas in the car from the pumps. Mom wasn't lying when she talked about how spread out Canada was. After we left our lunch spot we didn't see another place for hours. We finally found an abandoned motel a few hours from Prince George and stopped for the night. I was able to have a memoryless night that night, and we got back on the road in the morning. Mom's turn to drive today and I was in the back with Duke.

"How are we gonna get to the part in Alaska where it crosses over into Russia?" I asked, just crossing my mind. "I thought they didn't have a lot of roads up there before."

"Unfortunately, they don't still," Mom said. "There are some dirt roads though, and most of the rivers have probably dried up by now, so we can probably drive in those. We'll figure it out. It'll still be another day or two till we have to worry about that though."

"True," I said lightly and just watched out the window. The wilderness was gorgeous this far away from civilization. I could see elk and bison along the road. A wolf was in the road at one point.

Mom had to slow down to avoid hitting it. I was fascinated, it was all so amazing.

We made it all up to a little town called Prophet River before we stopped for the night. It must have been summertime, given the lack of snow, but also the extended daylight hours this far north. It had to have been almost nine at night, but the sun was just going down. We stopped at a small cabin off the main road back in the trees. I thought it could be someone's house, but the front door was off its hinges and it was missing a piece of the roof. I doubt someone would being living it in year 'round at least. We searched it of course and it was empty. There was only one bedroom, living room, kitchen, and bathroom. Mom insisted that Ally and I took the bedroom and she would take the couch. I reluctantly agreed but made sure Duke would stay out there with her, just in case.

* * *

I'm younger again, probably seven or eight. Taller than I was when Mandy died. I'm in a nice shirt and khaki shorts I have a backpack on and a lunch box in my hand. I'm standing on the front porch of our house, Mom is kneeling in front of me, fixing my hair.

"You look so handsome," she said, smiling. "You're first day of school. I'm so proud of my baby boy."

"Mom..." I hear myself whine and she laughs. "Can we go now?" I didn't like her fussing over me.

"Okay, okay," she said standing up and letting me run to the car ahead of me. I don't see dad; I assume he's working or something. Mom opens the back door for me to jump in and then climbs in the driver's seat herself. Turning to make sure I'm buckled, before pulling out of the driveway.

"I'm kinda scared," I said softly. "What if nobody likes me?" she smiled at me in the rearview mirror.

"They are gonna love you, baby," she said lightly. "You are a great little boy. You're gonna have friends lined up out the door." I laughed.

"I don't think so," I replied.

"Even if you don't make any friends today," she continued. "You have a whole year to make friends. And I'll be here to pick you up after school. You'll always have me. I'll always be your friend." She reached back and squeezed my leg a little and I smiled.

"I love you, Mom," I said and turned to watch out the window.

"I love you, honey."

Same outfit, same day by the looks of it, but after school. I'm running outside of the school and see my mom standing on the curb talking to some other moms. I automatically run to her and she turns just into time to catch me in her arms. I'm upset, though I don't remember why.

"What's a matter sweetheart?" She asked as she picked me up and carried me towards the car. I could feel her arm waving behind me, probably saying bye to the other moms.

"I didn't make any friends," I said, and I felt tears down my face.

"Aw," she said and ran her hand along my hair. "It's okay baby."

"I was so scared and couldn't talk to anyone," I cried. She opened the car door and set me in my seat in the back. "Nobody came to talk to me either. I'll never make any friends." She wiped the tears from my face.

"Yes, you will sweetheart," she said softly. "Maybe they were scared too. The first day can be scary for everyone. It'll be better tomorrow." She smiled and I tried to smile back, wiping my nose on my hand. "Besides you still have me. I'll always be your friend. You're stuck with me."

"Promise?" I asked, tears still brimming. "Promise you'll never leave me?"

"I promise, baby," she said and leaned in to kiss me on the forehead. "I'll never ever leave you my sweet boy."

* * *

I woke up on my own, the light flooding in through the window. I realized that I was alone, Ally was gone, and my first thought was panic. I jumped up and ripped open the bedroom door. Mom and Ally were sitting on the couch, obviously they had been talking, but cut short when I came out.

"You okay?" Ally asked, seeing my face.

"Yeah," I said. "Sorry, I kinda panicked when I woke up alone." I smiled shyly.

"I'm right here, babe," She said, patting the armrest next to her for me to come over. I walked over and perched on the armrest. I leaned down and kissed her forehead. "I wouldn't go far; I know you better than that." I chuckled and blushed a little. "Me and Mom were just in here talking and we figured we'd let you sleep in a bit."

"Well, thank you," I said, and Mom smiled at me. Something on her face made me ask, "What were you guys talking about?"

"Just girl talk," Ally said lightly and smiled up at me. I looked back at Mom and raised my eyebrows, but she just smiled. I know enough about women to not question 'girl talk.'

"Okay," I said, brushing it off.

"There's some breakfast on the stove if you're hungry, honey," Mom said, gesturing towards the small kitchen behind us. I finally noticed Duke there, eating his own breakfast and I smiled. I stood and went over and dished me up a bowl. I came back and sat in the armchair across from the couch.

"Thanks, Mom," I said and ate silently, hoping they would continue their 'girl talk,' curious what it involved. They didn't, obviously, it wasn't meant for me to know. I just focused on my food.

"Of course, my sweet boy. We'll head out when you're done," Mom said. I have a flash back to my memory of my first school day. I felt a warmth in my chest, glad that some emotions were returning to me regarding my mother.

"How long have you two been up?" I asked lightly.

"Just an hour or so," Ally replied. "We've already got the rest of the stuff loaded in the car, just gotta clean up breakfast and then we can go."

"Well, you guys have been busy," I said jokingly.

"We're big girls," Mom countered. "We can do all kinds of stuff." I held my hands up in mock surrender.

"I have no doubt about that," I said smiling.

"We should make it to the Alaskan border," Ally started, gesturing to Mom's map on the coffee table, I hadn't noticed earlier. "Or a least almost to it by the end of the day."

"Sounds good," I said finishing my food. "Let me grab my boots and stuff and I'll be ready to go." I stand up and kiss Ally on my way before dropping my bowl on the counter in the kitchen and head into the bedroom. I pulled my boots on and grabbed my pistol from under my pillow and rifle by the bed. I did a quick glance around the room making sure we didn't forget anything and headed back out.

CHAPTER 16

We loaded up in the car and headed out again. It will be nice to stay in one place for more than a night again. I feel myself craving that stability again, that safety. We haven't seen any people since we crossed into Canada, which is surprising for me. I expected to see some people at least, maybe run into some headhunters or something. I was, honestly, getting kind of bored, needing some sort of action. I smiled to myself at my own dirty thought, then reminded myself that we were travelling with my mother and that would be weird.

We made it to a town right before the Alaskan border a couple hours before nightfall, granted it was still almost 8. I hope we get through Alaska and back south quickly, I don't like this constant daylight thing. We shack up in another small cabin, still no people around. I'm starting to the assume that everyone headed south after the War. I kept my weapons close by just in case. One bedroom, which Ally and I insisted that Mom take tonight, I slept on the floor, with Ally on the couch, Duke with her at her feet. She was short enough, so they both fit easily. Ally had her hand hanging over the side of the couch, holding mine when we dosed off to sleep. I had gotten used to feeling her next to me, but this would have to do for tonight. As long as I had her close to me.

* * *

"I love her, Mom," I said. I'm older than the previous night's memories, high school age. I already know I'm talking about Ally. I'm standing in the living room, Mom and Dad sitting on the couch in front of me.

"I know you do," she said. "We all love her."

"No," I said, I was obviously frustrated, and resumed pacing that I knew I was doing earlier. "I'm *in love with her*." I emphasized each word, making my point. "I try to think of a life without her and I can't. It hurts to picture a future without her by my side. I know I'm going to marry her. I know I'm going to have kids with her. I know I'm going to grow old with her." Mom smiled and Dad leaned to get up.

"I think I'll let you handle this one, sweetheart," he said, kissing her on the cheek and patting me on the shoulder, leaving the room.

"My sweet boy," Mom said calmly, obviously thinking about how to talk to me about this. "Come sit down." She patted the seat Dad had just left. I flopped down on couch next to her. She put her leg up on the couch so she could turn to face me.

"I love her, Mom," I said, pinching my nose. "I don't know what to do."

"What do you mean?" she asked. "She knows you love her."

"No," I said. "She knows I care about her. I've never told her I was in love with her. I've never told her how I feel. I mean, I'm sure she has figured it out, but I've never *told her*."

"Why not?"

"I don't know," I sighed. "Maybe because I'm afraid she won't feel the same way." She laughed and I shot her a look.

"Baby, I'm not trying to be mean," she said reaching over and patting my leg. "I just think it's crazy to think that she wouldn't feel the same way. You guys have been inseparable since you two met in fifth grade. Why do you think she wouldn't feel the same way?"

"I don't know," I said softly, staring at my hands in my lap. "I'm scared. I love her so much and I feel pain thinking about losing her. I'm scared that if she doesn't feel the same way that I'll lose her." Mom sighed.

"Honey," she started. "Relationships are hard for everyone. Especially first loves. Hell, I could tell you some stories about boys I was with before your father and I'm sure he has a few too." I glanced at her sideways. "No, your father was not my first love, nor was I his." She sighed again before continuing. "Love is a complicated emotion sweetheart. You love different people different ways. I love your father, and I love you, but they're not the same type of love, if that makes sense. You love Ally. Ally loves you. Yes, I know you mean you're in love with her and I understand that. But I think you'll be surprised if you just open up to her and talk to her."

"What if she doesn't feel the same way? What if she sees me as less of a man if I'm honest?"

"Baby," she reached over for my hand and I took hers, turning to look at her. "Being a man is about more than strength, physical or emotional. Hell being human is about more that. Just because you're a man, doesn't mean you don't have human emotions. Like love or fear or sadness or insecurities or depression or anything like that. Being a man is being able to be the manly man, the protector, but also being able to cry in front of the woman you love or someone you care about. You think your father hasn't cried with me? That he hasn't talked to me about things that make him sad or depressed? That he's just this rock all the time?"

"Well, I guess," I shrugged.

"Sweetie," she said softly. "I've seen your father cry many times before. He has cried on my shoulder while I comforted him, and I have cried on his shoulder. Being in love with someone is about being able to be yourself with that person. Being able to be vulnerable, being able to cry or laugh or just sit in silence with them comfortably. You and Ally are amazing together and you've been there for her through all that stuff with her foster dad. You are her rock but being in love with someone is about being more than a rock for each other when it's needed. You have to let yourself be vulnerable to her. You can't just pretend to be this rock for her and pretend you don't have emotions. For one, I bet she'll see right through it." I laughed. "More importantly, it's about opening up and letting her see who you are on the inside. If you keep trying to be this knight in shining armor for her with no emotions, she's going to pull away from you. You would have her on this pedestal and be protecting her, but not allowing her to protect you too."

"But—"

"I'm not talking in a fight or something," she said quickly. "She doesn't have to physically protect you to protect you. I mean like with your emotions, your thoughts, your fears, your insecurities, everything that makes you, you. Because if you continue to hold all that inside yourself, you're going to burn yourself out and end up pushing her away without meaning to. To be quite honest, that's what happened with me and your father after Mandy died." I looked at her again, surprised.

"Yes," she said. "You knew we had problems, and that's what caused some of them. He shut me out and tried to deal with his grief on his own. He wanted to help me through mine, but not show his, not show that he was hurting too. Granted I wasn't pushing for it, because I was dealing with my own grief, but on the outside I saw him as not being affected by it and it made me pull away from him. He was trying so hard to be there for me and you but was trying to deal with his own issues on his own. We obviously have gotten better after counselling, but that's why I'm telling you all this. If you truly love her, you have to let her in.

You have to let your walls come down and let her see your heart, your feelings for her. You don't want to have to go to counselling years later to try to fix habits that are hard to break. You two are already so close. If you let her in, I'm sure you will get even closer. I can see you getting married and having kids and growing old together. You have to start that kind of relationship with honesty on both sides, honey. Does that make sense?" I nodded slowly.

"Yes," I said. "It makes sense Mom. But how do I bring it up? How do I show her that I love her? How do I tell her?"

"You'll feel it," she said. "You've felt it before I'm sure when you figured out you had these feelings for her, but I'm betting you pushed them down and shut them away, because you were afraid. That's one of those hard to break habits I'm talking about. You have to just let it out. You have to just tell her. Next time you're with her and you two are just sitting there together and you feel it, say it. Don't shove in that bottle in your chest. That's the first step. As for your fear of her not feeling the same way, I've seen the way she looks at you honey. I guarantee you she feels the same way. It's how I used to look at your father when we were first dating. Hell, I still look at him that way even now."

"What did Dad do when he first told you he loved you?" I asked, and she smiled.

"He stuttered a lot and it took him a minute to get it out," she said, and I laughed at the thought. "It was so cute and adorable. He gave me his class ring too. Said it was a promise to our future together." I heard the front door open and none other than Ally walked in the door, a smile on her face. Her smile faltered when she saw my face.

"Hey Al," I said, smiling at her.

"Hey," she said. "Hi Mom. Everything okay?"

"Of course, sweetie," Mom said, smiling her. "We're just having a chat. Why don't you head on downstairs and Leo will be down there in a bit?" Ally nodded and locked eyes with me, I smiled, and she smiled back, heading down the stairs.

"Thanks, Mom," I said, leaning over and giving her a hug. "I love you."

"I love you, my sweet boy," she said. "Go on, your girl is waiting." I laughed and headed down the stairs myself.

* * *

I woke up when Duke jumped off the couch and stepped on my foot. At first, I thought he had heard something, but he just headed into the kitchen to get a drink of water. I laid my head back down and looked up at Ally above me on the couch. She was still asleep. She looked so peaceful while she slept. I decided to let her sleep and stood up to use the bathroom. Coming back out I saw that the door to the bedroom was open, I peaked in and saw it empty. I cocked my head to the side wondering where Mom was, when I saw movement outside the front window on the porch. I headed to the front door and stepped outside, shutting the door quietly behind me, as to not wake Ally.

"Hey, baby," Mom said. She was sitting in one of the two chairs on the porch, watching the sun come up. "I found some coffee." She held up the mug in her hands. "There's still some left if you want some inside."

"I'm okay for now," I said sitting in the chair beside her. We just watched the sun come up over the trees in front of us. It was beautiful, peaceful.

"You okay, honey?" She asked looking at me, obviously seeing my wheels turning.

"I've had a couple memories come back," I said.

"Oh?"

"My first day of school where I was upset that I didn't make any friends," I said, and she smiled. "You promising to never ever leave me. And then just now, the conversation I had with you about trying to figure out how to tell Ally I was in love with her."

"That was a deep conversation," She said thoughtfully, sipping her coffee. I laughed.

"Yeah," I agreed. "It sure was. But even without my memories, a lot of what you said has stuck with me through the years. I guess my subconscious really liked what you told me." She chuckled.

"I'm glad," she said. "It was probably the best advice I ever gave you." I laughed. "Especially seeing you with her now. Like when you had your little breakdown the other morning." I looked down at my hands.

"That was when I remembered the day Mandy died in the hospital," I said softly, and she was quiet. "I guess it hit me a little harder than I expected it to."

"It still hits me hard too," she said. "I'm so proud of the man you've grown up to be, my sweet boy. You've learned to balance the soft side with the hard side, and I can tell that Ally is proud of you too. And I'm so proud that you two have grown together even more so than when you were kids. You're closer than you've ever been before. I guess some of that advise stuck." I laughed a little.

"I'm sorry I've been kind of distant with you, Mom," I said. "Not being able to remember the feelings related to you has been hard for me. Like obviously, I knew you were Mom, but knowing it and feeling it were entirely different."

"Don't apologize, sweetie," She said softly, and patted my hand. "It wasn't your fault. I didn't want to push you, because I knew you didn't remember. I wanted you to remember on your own."

"Ally had said the same when I first started getting my memories back," I said. "I may not remember everything, but that first day of school and that conversation about love. I know that you mean everything to me Mom. I know that you'll never leave me." I was staring at my hands, but I could see her wipe a tear from her eye out of my peripheral vision.

"Never ever, my sweet boy," she said, reaching over and squeezing my hand. I squeezed back and we sat there watching the sun finally break over the treetops. I breathed in the fresh air and enjoyed the quiet.

The front door opened behind me and Duke bolted out, running around the grass in front of the deck, sniffing around for a spot to relieve himself. Ally stepped out of the door and shut it behind her. She had a coffee mug in her hands.

"There you guys are," she said, sitting down on my leg and giving me a kiss. I wrapped my arm around her back, and she leaned into me.

"We're enjoying the sunrise," Mom said, sipping her coffee. "See you found the good stuff." She raised her mug to Ally and Ally raised hers back.

"Yes, ma'am," she said lightly. "Thank you for that by the way. I haven't had coffee in a long time."

"No problem," Mom replied. "There's some grounds left too; we're so taking them along. I missed coffee." I laughed.

"You girls and your coffee," I said, and Ally offered me her mug. I took a sip, it tasted stale, but it worked.

"You love it too," Ally countered. "You and I used to get coffee on the way to school."

"Really?" I asked, I hadn't remembered that. I knew I liked coffee, obviously, given the experiment, but still.

"Yep," Ally said. "I got you into it. You didn't like it till I made you try mine and then you started getting some too." I laughed.

"Peer pressure. Got it." I said, and Mom laughed.

CHAPTER 17

The trip through Alaska and Russia was interesting. We had been able to stock up in Fairbanks again. Most of Alaska had been left untouched from the War. We saw a few people there, but other than that, we hadn't seen anyone else in days. Past Fairbanks we had to drive along rivers and what used to be smaller creeks that had dried up. The bigger rivers had receded enough to allow us to drive on the banks without too many issues. Russia had been more of the same, hardly any people, driving through old rivers and creek beds. We were finally able to make it back on roads about halfway down towards Mongolia. We had decided to avoid the coast in China, due to it being so highly populated before the War. We figured it would be either bombed or overpopulated and unsafe either way. We decided to go through Mongolia and cut down the middle of China, that was more sparse than the coast.
It was nice to see some buildings again, compared to the wilderness that was Alaska and Russia. Granted, it was gorgeous, but it was nice to have the possibility of seeing people again, kind of a reminder that we weren't alone in the world. We stopped in a small town, still in Russia, but almost to the Mongolian border.

We found a small, shack, for lack of a better word, to sleep for the night. It's one room, so we're all laid on the floor, close together. I laid there beside Ally with Mom on her other side and Duke near our feet. I was staring at the ceiling, listening to the sounds outside. We hadn't seen anyone in this small town, but of course I was still cautious. Mom and Ally were asleep, and Duke hadn't moved at all, so I assumed he hadn't heard anything either. I nestled in closer to Ally and tried to sleep.

* * *

I'm high school age again, probably 16 or so. I'm standing in our kitchen; mom is sitting at the table looking at me. She looks concerned and I felt angry, so I knew I had probably been talking to her about something.

"She was crying again last night," I said angrily. I must be talking about Ally again. "Her foster mom treats her like shit. Her foster dad ignores her now, yes, but she just feels so alone. She hates living there. I don't understand why you guys can't just adopt her!" I throw my hands up, frustrated.

"Honey," Mom said calmly. "We've looked into it; we can't do that."

"Well, why not?!"

"Do you want to spend your life with her?" she asked, and I'm surprised by the question.

"Yes, you know I do," I said flatly.

"Then we can't adopt her," she said softly, and I cocked my head to the side, confused. "Come sit down." I sat down in the chair opposite of her and sighed.

"I don't understand," I said.

"We looked into it," she said. "If you want to continue to have a romantic relationship we can't adopt her. If we adopt her you would be legally siblings at that point. Which means you can't be with her like that. It would be illegal; they investigate all that stuff before they let someone adopt a child. If they find out that you two have that kind of relationship they definitely wouldn't let us adopt her. Then you wouldn't be able to marry her in the future either, because you would legally siblings."

"Oh," I said, defeated.

"Why do you think we've let her come over here all the time when she wants?" Mom asked. "Why do you think we gave her a key to the house? We are perfectly okay with her being over here all the time, whenever she wants to be, but we cannot make it legal if you two are together. I'm sorry, honey, but it just wouldn't be a good idea."

"That actually makes sense," I said softly.

"I know," she said. "That's what I thought when they told us. That's why we decided not to do it."

"Well can I marry her when we turn 18?" I asked and she smiled.

"You'd have to wait till she turns 18," she said. "But yes, honey. We can have the wedding the day after her birthday if you want. That way she'll be an official part of our family, but you two could still be together."

"Okay," I said, relieved.

"Hon," Dad had just walked into the kitchen. "You ready to go to the store?" We both stood up and Mom hugged me.

"Ally will be over in a bit," I said.

"That's fine by me," she said, and smiled. "We'll be back in a couple hours. I love you."

"I love you, Mom."

* * *

I wake up and it's still dark outside. I'm not sure what time it is or what woke me up though. Ally and Mom are still asleep, and Duke hasn't moved from his spot by our feet. I laid my head back down and stared at the ceiling, thinking back to the memory. I realize that was the last time I saw my parents before the bombs dropped. The last time I saw my dad alive. I sighed, playing the memory back again. Obviously, Ally and I hadn't gotten married the day after her 18th birthday, but it was nice to know that my parents supported our relationship that much.

I must have fallen asleep again, because when I woke again, Ally and Mom were up and moving around the room. I smelled salmon and was glad that we had been able to get some canned salmon in Fairbanks. Pork and beans had been getting a little old. I got up and went outside to use the bathroom. The downfall to being in a small town in a foreign country; indoor plumbing wasn't a thing here, I guess.

"Smells good," I said, walking back inside and kissing Ally.

"Definitely better than pork and beans," Mom said as she dished us up our food. We laughed.

After we ate, we packed up again and headed out. We had a routine by now after a week on the road. I had had a few small memories come back over that time. I remember our first dog was a beagle named Oliver. I remembered being in a pool with Ally and other people our age. She had explained that was one of our high school friend's birthday party. I remember a school dance with Ally in middle school. I remember going to a baseball game with my dad. It was nice to have some of the little stuff come back too, filling in the gaps.

I was driving, we came over a hill and I'm immediately pulled from my thoughts. There were people standing in the road, vehicles blocking our way. I slammed on the breaks to avoid hitting them. There were buildings all around us, that we hadn't seen before the hill. Mom in the back leaned forward looking at the people in front of us, Duke barked.

"Headhunters," Mom said, and I tensed up.

"What do we do?" Ally asked.

"Just stay calm," Mom said. "We can talk to them. They're not uncivilized." I looked back at her, skeptical. Ally looked calmer than me and put her hand on my thigh. The people had walked to our car by this point. They had dirty clothes, and I saw a bone on the necklaces they wore. I'm assuming a human bone, maybe their symbol for being a headhunter. The one closest to my door had his rifle trained on me. I kept my hands on the wheel.

"Get out," He shouted. "Slowly. I wanna see your hands." Duke growled.

"It's okay, Duke," Ally said softly, he stopped growling, but still didn't look comfortable.

"Now!" the man shouted again. I reached and put the car in park and opened my door. Ally and Mom followed suit and we all slowly got out of the vehicle, our hands raised. There were six men around us, all armed, all wearing a bone around their necks. I didn't like these odds but stayed quiet.

"We simply seek passage through your territory," Mom said, confidently, but friendly. The man who had shouted looked at her, rifle still trained on me.

"Why would we grant you passage?" he asked sharply.

"Your rules state that if someone requests passage, and is not hostile, their request should at least be considered, if not allowed," Mom said in a very authoritative voice. The man's look faltered and mine did as well. I looked at her, but she continued to look at the man. She obviously had more knowledge about these people than she had let on.

"Where did you hear that?" He sneered, trying to regain his composure.

"From the tribe I lived with where we are from," she said matter-of-factly. "I learned your ways and your rules. If you will not grant us passage, we request audience with your tribe elder to request it from them." The man hesitated, but I could see the wheels turning in his head. Mom obviously had experience and understanding about how their hierarchy worked. I had so many questions for her but knew this wasn't the time or place.

"Fine," he said finally. "You will leave all weapons here in your vehicle." Mom nodded and began pulling weapons from her person, setting them in the back seat of the car. I hesitated but followed suit when I saw Ally catch my eye. She nodded and I knew she knew more than me too. After I had pulled all the weapons from my person and set them in the front seat, I reached in and turned off the car, taking the keys with me. I stood and closed the door.

"Search them," he said to the other men around him. A few lowered their weapons and began patting us down. They didn't trust us to do as we were told. When they were satisfied that we were unarmed the man turned and headed towards the closest building. Mom followed and Ally, and I fell into step behind her with Duke tagging along beside her. I felt her squeeze my hand in reassurance. Two of the other men followed behind us, while to the others stayed at their post on the road.

"You're in luck," the man said to Mom, I strained to listen. "One of our grand elders is here. He has been traveling. He will be able to assess if you know all that you say you do."

"I will gladly answer any questions he has for us," Mom said calmly, but still very authoritative. I was in awe and confusion, but I know we are at a disadvantage here, so I'll let her do what she knows.

"Good," the man grunts as he walks up the steps to the building. We go inside and I realize it reminds me of a town hall meeting place. About the size of a small church, open with two tables along the walls to either side. There is another table at the end of room, two men are sitting at it, they look up at us when we enter.

"What is this?" The younger of the two asked. He was probably around my mother's age, shaggy hair and a beard. He looked rugged, but strong. The older one was grayer and more fragile looking. The man who brought us here, bowed slightly and then stepped to the side, to gesture towards us.

"These people have—" he started, but the rugged man stood up at the sight of my mother.

"Carol?" he said, stepping towards her, she took a step back.

"How do you know me?" she asked. The man smiled and chuckled a little.

"I'm sure I look a little different than the last time we saw each other," he said almost sweetly to her. I was confused. "It's me, David."

"David?" Mom asked, obviously surprised. She took a step closer to him, looking him over. I saw recognition in her eyes as they lit up. "David!" She automatically hugged him, and I was even more confused.

CHAPTER 18

"Uh," I said, looking at them and then Ally. Ally smiled at me, a telling smile. She knew about David. "Who's David?" Mom pulled back from David and looked at me sheepishly. The men who brought us in were also confused, looking at each other.

"You're dismissed," David said to them sternly. They still looked confused but left us here with David. Even the older man got up and left the room.

"Mom?" I asked and for the first time, she looked embarrassed. Ally stepped up at that point.

"Maybe we should give them some time to talk," she said to me and pulled at my hand to walk me away from them. I stood my ground.

"I'm not leaving her here with him," I said, and I saw a flash of something I didn't recognize on David's face. Ally reached up and turned my face back towards her.

"Trust me, babe," she said sternly, and I could tell that she trusted this David guy to not hurt my mom. I sighed and let her pull me back the way we came.

"We'll be just outside," I said over my shoulder. We went outside the door and Ally sat down on the steps of the building. I could see the men had resumed their position over on the road, but they were watching us. Duke sat beside Ally, still not sure of what to make of everything, but staying close regardless.

"What the hell is going on?" I asked her, frustrated. "Who is that guy?" She took my pulled me down to sit beside her.

"Babe," she started. "Relax. David is probably the last person that would ever hurt your mom." I just stared at her and she sighed. "You remember the other day? When I said that Mom and I were having girl talk?"

"Yes."

"She went into more details about what had happened to her in the time since she got out of the bunker to when she met up with us. That included David."

"Wait. What?" I said, still lost.

"She was out on her own and ended up almost dying at one point. She was taken in by some people, they were almost Wiccan. Believed in Mother Earth and being one with the Earth and all that. They helped her get healthy again and she stayed with them for a while. Learning about them and what they believed in. Some of them had had dealings with headhunters before and their group kind of meshed together with them—"

"Wait, how does respecting Mother Earth and all mesh with cannibalism?"

"Mom explained it all to me. They're not cannibals, well not in the sense that we know cannibals. Yes, they eat humans sometimes, but it's more than that. Their groups or tribes started as a rebellion from the military. Apparently, a lot of them had worked for the military before the War but they basically got screwed over by the military at some point. So, they formed this group against them, and it took off from there. The cannibalism came in later when they were short on food supplies. It's not like what we remember of savage people that just bite people's legs and things." I laughed. "A lot of them have medical backgrounds, from the military and whatnot. The Wiccans came into it because they hated what the military had done to the Earth. So, they joined up somewhat, sharing survival tips and things."

"So, Mom was with the Wiccans at the time they went to the headhunters. David was there. Mom of course was alone and lonely. She and David got to talking and they fell in love." I scoffed.

"How can mom fall for a cannibal?" I snapped.

"Because he's more than that," she said calmly. "Not all of them eat human, nor are they required to, babe. He is, apparently, a good man. He had lost his wife and son in the bombings and blamed the military. I don't know exactly why, but he basically formed this whole headhunter thing. Or was one of the ones who started it up. Obviously, it's expanded over the years. I mean, we're in Asia, come on. They spent quite a few years together from what Mom said. He wanted to travel, to visit the other tribes, but Mom wouldn't leave the area because she was waiting to see if we made it out. He understood, but he had to go, so he left. She thought he was probably dead but had told me it was a possibility that we might hear about him or even run into him if he had survived."

"Why didn't she tell me any of this?"

"She was concerned on how you would react," she said, simply. "Not only because of the whole cannibal thing—which you really have to get past, babe—but also, the fact that this was another man that your mother fell in love with. After your dad, she didn't want to put you through that story, if we never ran into him or anything. Especially with your memories not all there. She didn't want you to feel like she didn't love your dad or that she was forgetting about him or you." I stared at our hands, thinking.

"I know she loved Dad," I said. "That she still loves him."

"Yes. Now," she said. "But how would you have felt when we first found her, and she tells you about this man that she's in love with?"

"Okay, that's fair," I said. "But I mean, I get it. We're all out here in this world without the people from our past. There's bound to be connections made and maybe even love with people you do find out here. A headhunter? Wait, does that mean Mom is a cannibal?" Ally laughed.

"No," she said. "Of course, I asked if she had tried it. She said she could never bring herself to try it. That's when she explained that it's not required and not everyone does it. That it was more of a once-in-a-while thing, but that they let people run with the rumor, that way they'll be left alone. They have rules, a hierarchy, and hell David is a grand elder. Think of it more in terms of like the Native American tribes we learned about in school. They have rituals and they believe that the Earth will provide. Hence, how the Wiccans got involved. Granted, yes, sometimes it's human that it provides. The way Mom explained it, they're actually very civilized and caring people. Like a big family that's spread out over the world." I sat there, still staring at our hands, absentmindedly running my thumb over the back of her hand.

"I still don't trust him," I said flatly, and she sighed again. "Not because of the whole cannibal thing. Just that's my mom, you know. I can't just trust some random guy that knew her years ago. Dad wouldn't want that. I know he would want her to be happy, but he would want me to make sure she was safe. Does that make sense?"

"Yes, baby," she said, reaching up and stroking my cheek. "I know what you mean. We aren't going to just leave her here with him. I doubt she would want to stay here with him if we left. She was set to go to Australia with us and she was under the impression that he was dead. Mom wouldn't just let us go off alone without knowing that we're safe. You know that."

"I know," I said, leaning into her hand.

"You have to realize that Mom is a woman with feelings," she said. "She loves him. I could see it when she talked about him. You have to respect that. She was alone for so long, but she had him. Now she has him back, but she also doesn't want to lose you again either. I'm not saying go call him 'Dad' and play catch with him." I laughed. "You just have to respect that Mom has a life too." I nodded.

"I know I know," I said, sighing. "How long has it been since he left?"

"About two years from what Mom said. He wanted her to go with him of course, but she wouldn't leave the area without us. He said he understood, but that he would find her again. That they would be together again." I groaned. "Oh, come on, that was cute. That would be something you would say to me."

"I know, but that's my mom. It's weird." She laughed.

"You're a dork," she said leaning in to kiss me. I heard the door open behind us and Mom and David walked out. I immediately saw they were holding hands, Mom looked happy, but cautious when she looked at me.

"David said we could stay here tonight," she said slowly, watching me for a reaction. I only nodded.

"It'll be nice to spend the day somewhere instead of on the road," Ally said, squeezing my hand and I nodded again and stood up.

"Excuse me," David said. "I need to go talk to my men." He leaned down and kissed Mom on the cheek. Anger flared in me, but I would have to give him a chance. He walked away and Mom looked at me.

"I'm sure you have a lot of questions," she said softly.

"Yes, I do," I replied.

"He's cute," Ally chimed in. I groaned and rolled my eyes. Mom laughed. Good, the tension was broken. Mom gestured back towards the building.

"Come on," she said, leading the way back inside. "We can sit down and talk."

We all wander back inside and sit at the table that David and the older man were at earlier.

"Ally told me about what you two talked about," I started.

"Good," Mom said. "I figured she would."

"I get it," I said. "I do. Love can come from anywhere. But I don't think I'll trust him right off the bat Mom. Dad would kill me." She laughed.

"I don't expect you to, Leo," she said. "But he is a good man. I spent years with him before you two got out. I understand it's going to take some getting used to. You know I wouldn't bring someone into my life or your life without me trusting them."

"Does he make you happy?" I asked and I could tell she was surprised by the question.

"Yes," she said. "Yes, he does. You know I will always love your father. My love for David will never replace my love for Matt. Just like his love for me will never replace his love for Jill."

"Jill was his wife I'm assuming?"

"Yes," she said. "She and their son, Ethan, died in the bombings. He would have been about your age by now. David said you already remind him of Ethan." That must have been the look he had earlier. I feel a twinge of sadness for David.

"How does he feel about all this?" I asked.

"He loves me and wants to be with me, of course," she said. "But he knows that you and Ally are my priority. He actually mentioned that he would be happy to escort us to Australia. He has plenty of connections all over Asia. He could make sure we got there safe."

"What do you mean 'escort us?'" Ally asked.

"He said he would understand if you didn't want him to stick around after we got there," she said looking at me. "That he would be willingly to leave after he knew I was safe, if it made you uncomfortable." I felt a stab of guilt at that point. I couldn't ask my mother to give up her love again for me. Though I had more respect for him too, to be willing to leave the woman you love if it made her happy, by making me happy. He understood the relationship.

"Mom," I said slowly. "I may not trust him right now, but if he makes you happy, I can't ask you to give him up for me again. You stayed when he left for me, I'm sure that hurt. I would be selfish to put my feelings above yours. You deserve happiness too. I can grow to trust him, probably." Mom smiled with tears in her eyes, Ally even wiped her own eyes. "I may be cautious, but I'm not an asshole." We all laughed.

The door opened and David walked back in. I stood and approached him, extending my hand.

"I think it's time we were properly introduced," I said, strongly. "I'm Leo." He smiled behind his beard and shook my hand.

"David," he said. "I've heard a lot about you."

"I, unfortunately, have only just now heard about you," I said, glancing at Mom and smiling. She covered her face and laughed. "I apologize for my reaction earlier."

"It's okay," he said, smiling again. "I totally understand." Ally came to my side and shook David's hand as well.

"I'm Ally," she said. "Whatever Mom said about me was probably all lies." We all laughed.

"Oh, come on," Mom called, coming over and wrapping an arm around David's waist. It was weird to see, but I didn't say anything. I would have to get used to it; Mom deserved to be happy too. "I would only ever tell him the good stuff." David glanced behind us to Duke, who came over and was sniffing at David's feet. He reached his hand down so Duke could smell it.

"And who's this?" he asked.

"That's Duke," Ally said. "We found him on the road when he was eating our leftover dinner one night." David laughed. Duke seemed satisfied with sniffing and licked David's hand and let him pet his head. I guess if Duke trusts him, I could work on trusting him.

"If you guys want to move your car I can show you where you guys can stay for the night," David said, steering Mom towards the door and leading the way. "My men know you're my guests, they won't mess with you. If you have any issues at all, just let me know." He really was in charge, I guess.

He led the way outside and turned to walk around the building, towards some of the smaller buildings. Houses, sort of, 'huts' was a more accurate description. They were made of what looked like sticks and some type of big leaves. The main building, we just came from was similar in construction, but looked sturdier.

He took us to one off to the left and opened the door. Inside was a mud stove of sorts with a fire burning inside it. A small table with a couple chairs and a bed that was made of more leaves, but had a wood frame, so it was off the floor.

"It's not what you're probably used to," David said, with an arm still around Mom. "But it's more comfortable than it looks." I laughed.

"It'll work," Ally said with a smile. My first thought was where would Mom be sleeping then, but then I realized she would probably stay with David. Still weird, but I force myself to be calm about it.

"Mine is over there," David said, pointing to another hut about 100 yards off to the right. "You can bring your car over here so it's not sitting in the road. If you need anything, just let me know. We'll probably have lunch in a couple hours." I must have made a face, because he added. "Don't worry, we're having elk." He smiled and I laughed, a little embarrassed.

"I'll see you guys later," Mom said, smiling at me and squeezing my hand. She and David turned and headed for his hut. I looked over at Ally, she was watching my face.

"Still weird," I said, flatly, once they were out of earshot. She laughed and pulled my hand back towards the car.

"Come on, let's move the car," she said. Duke was running around sniffing everywhere, marking his territory.

We moved the car over by our hut. The men over there watched us the whole time but didn't say anything. I decided to try out the bed and he was right; it was more comfortable than it looked. Duke turned in a circle a few times before settling on the floor by the mud stove. Ally kicked off her shoes and laid down next to me, her head on my chest. I had one hand behind my head and the other around Ally, tracing circles on her back.

"You okay?" She asked.

"Yeah," I said. "Just thinking about David and Mom. And about the memory I had last night. I haven't had a chance to tell you about it. It was the last conversation I had with Mom before the bombs fell. It was about why they wouldn't adopt you." She raised her head and looked at me.

"Really?" she asked. "You never told me about that."

"Well I guess I never really had a chance to," I said. "It was right before they left for the store that day. I was frustrated because you had been crying the night before. I asked Mom why they couldn't just adopt you. She said if they did, that you and I couldn't be together anymore. We would be legally siblings at that point, and we wouldn't be able to get married or anything."

"Wow," she said. "I never thought about that."

"Me either," I said, honestly. "She said that's why they gave you a key and didn't mind you being over at the house all the time. That they couldn't make it legal. I asked if we could just get married when we hit 18 then, that way you would be officially part of the family. She said we could have the wedding the day after your birthday if we wanted." She smiled.

"We'll get married one day," she said, probably feeling the way I did that we couldn't do it then. "But even if we don't, I'll always be yours."

"And I yours," I said. She smiled and kissed me. I hugged her tighter to me. "I love you with every fiber in my being, Al."

"I know," she said. "You've had my heart since 8th grade." I laughed.

"Really?" I asked. "That long?" She rolled over on her stomach, propping herself up on her arms so she could look at me.

"You remember when you gave me your class ring? The first time you said you loved me?" She asked and I nodded. "Well you weren't the first one to say it after all." I roll onto my side, propping my head up on my hand.

"How do you mean? I don't remember you ever saying it before that."

"Well you wouldn't," she said, blushing slightly. "Even if you had all your memories. We were in 8th grade, it was after that dance that you remembered the other day. I was over and we were lying in bed and you had fallen asleep first and I was kind of just watching you."

"Creeper," I joked, and she hit my chest.

"Shut up," she said. "Anyway, you were sleeping, and I was laying there looking at you and I said it out loud. You rolled over at that point and I thought you were awake and had heard me, but you just put your arm around me and slept on. Part of me felt like your subconscious heard me and wanted to be closer to me." I smiled. "But I said it first. I knew in that moment that I loved you with everything I was. Of course, I could tell you felt the same way, but I didn't want to push you. When you finally said it in high school, I wanted to cry."

"You know I actually remember a conversation with Mom the

day I gave you my class ring," I said. "I was frustrated, because I knew I was in love with you, but was scared that you didn't feel the same way. I talked to Mom and she talked about me needing to let my walls down, to let you in. That I couldn't always just be your rock, that I had to let you be my rock too." She smiled. "She talked about how after Mandy died, that Dad kind of shut her out and was trying to just deal with his stuff on his own and be there for her and me. She said that it made her pull away from him. She told me that if I wanted to make sure I didn't unintentionally push you away, that I had to show you that I could be vulnerable too. I told her I was worried you wouldn't see me as manly. She told me that being a man was about more than just being big and strong. It was about showing the person you love and people you care about that you're human too. She told me that the next time I was with you and I felt it, I should just say it. So, I did. I was scared to death." She laughed.

"You're so cute," she said and leaned in to kiss me. "Though I really don't know why you wouldn't think I felt the same way. I practically worshipped you."

"I know," I said. "Though, don't take this the wrong way, but I think now, thinking back on it, that I was scared that I was just your rock for everything going on with Jim and everything. And that when you finally got away from him, that you wouldn't need me anymore. I think I was scared that I was falling for a girl that only saw me as a knight in shining armor. If that makes sense."

"It does," she said. "But you weren't just my knight. You were my prince charming. Yes, you saved me, to be quite honest, I don't think I would have lived much longer if I hadn't met you and your family. You weren't just someone saving me. You showed me that I was worthy of love. That I wasn't just this plaything for someone. That I could be more than that. That I could be who I was meant to be. That I had a future. I never thought I did before that. I thought I would die in that house. Even at that young of an age, I felt like my life would never get better. That I would either be killed by him or kill myself. You opened my eyes to love and happiness and hope. You and your parents showed me how the world was supposed to be and that it was so much bigger than I realized." I was speechless. I reached out and caressed her face.

"I honestly don't know what to say, Al," I whispered, I felt a lump in my throat. "I never knew you felt that way. Though I'm glad you didn't die in that house."

"I've never told you," she said, kissing my palm, tears fell from her eyes. "Hell, I've never told anyone that… When I was getting all these memories back, it was all out of order like yours. Luckily, I got some back about you before the ones with Jim. I feel like if it was the other way around, I would have felt that same way again. Even when I did get some of those bad memories back, I held your class ring and just laid in bed, trying to picture your face." I felt a wave of guilt again for not being there for her. I pulled her to me and wrapped my arms around her.

"I'm so sorry that I wasn't there," I whispered in her ear, she was crying harder and I was fighting that lump in my throat. "I know I couldn't have been, but that doesn't matter. You never have to go through anything alone ever again, baby. I'm so sorry." I stroked her hair and held her tightly.

"You have no idea how hard it was for me when you first got out of the experiment," she said softly. "To not just run into your arms and break down and let everything just crash down again. You were there, but I knew I couldn't do that to you. It would have thrown you for a loop. I cried after I left your room that day, when you said you felt like you knew me. I couldn't stay away from you for long though, that's why I went and found you in the gym. Just being around you was helping, but it was killing me to not be able to run into your arms."

"I probably wouldn't have complained," I said lightly, and she laughed, pulling back and pressing her forehead against mine.

"You let a lot of girls you just met just run into your arms like that?"

"Only if they're cute," I said, smirking. She slapped my arm.

"These arms are spoken for," she said, I smiled, and kissed her. I pressed my forehead to hers again, my arms wrapped around her. We stayed like that in silence for a few minutes.

"Can we just stay like this forever?" I whispered.

"I'm in," she said. "Though we'll have to have bathroom breaks. And maybe snacks." I laughed.

"I love you," I said.

"I love you."

CHAPTER 19

The rest of the day was spent around mom and David, and the rest of the tribe. There were a lot more of them than I had realized when we got there. Lunch was in the middle of the group of buildings, away from the road. There was an elk roasting over a fire, there was rice, it was good. I spent a lot of time watching Mom with David. She looked so comfortable with him; they were talking and laughing with the other people in the tribe. It really showed that they had known each other for years. There were people around Ally and I too, though Ally did most of the talking. She was a good buffer for me, given I wasn't entirely comfortable around new people. Let alone people like this. There were children around and they loved Duke, he had warmed up quickly to them and was playing fetch with them. It was nice, it really felt like a family, though a weird one.

Later that day at dinner in the main building, the children were outside playing still, a few women out there watching them. It felt more formal in a way. David and Mom were at the head table, and Ally and I were at another table with people closer to our age. I actually joined in on the conversations, feeling a bit more comfortable here, Ally would put her hand on my back or pat my leg in reassurance occasionally. We talked about where we came from, from the military bunker and how we escaped. They asked about the people we left behind. I told them what I had told Ally, that I wanted to help them, but I didn't want to do anything stupid to just be heroic. They understood and spoke of their beliefs and wanting to liberate all the bunkers that were like that. Apparently, it wasn't just in the US, it was all over the world, the militaries of the world still thinking in terms of world domination. That they wanted as many people as they could get to take the rest of the world down. I guess the whole environment hasn't changed, even after the War. It made me angry.

They explained that that was the purpose of the whole headhunter idea. That it was about bringing humanity back together, to be together, and not to fight each other. Given there was so few people in the world, compared to before the War, we all needed to be together to help restore the planet and humanity. It made sense to me, I even agreed with it completely. I joked that the human-eating thing didn't sit right with me. They laughed, which I was surprised at. They explained that it had been years since anyone had had human and many of them admitted that they had never tried it. They confirmed what Ally had told me. That it was more of a rumor that they just let people run with. Especially early on, before they had the numbers and the stability to expand their ideas and beliefs. During that time, it was about survival, so they knew the rumors would keep people at bay. Even most of the bones that they all wore, weren't human, but animal bones. I lightened up more after that, realizing that these people were good people, that they were just like us.

After dinner, Mom and David said goodnight and went to his hut. Ally and I went to ours and I fell asleep easily, feeling almost safe with these people. It had been a while since I had felt that way.

The next morning when we were packing up to leave a few of the people around mine and Ally's age came over to us. They gave us each a necklace with a bone on it. They assured me that the bones were from an elk, to which I laughed. They said it was so that we would remember all that we learned from them and what we were all fighting for. That it would also help us along the way with other tribes we ran into. We thanked them and shook hands; Ally even gave them hugs. They wished us safe travels and hoped that we would return one day.

Later, David driving, Mom in the front, Duke, Ally, and I crammed in the backseat. We needed to find a bigger car, I guess. It was quiet for the most part, but Mom asked about what we thought of the tribe.

"I like them," I said, honestly. She looked at me surprised. "I know. But the people we talked to last night at dinner explained that it's all about trying to bring humanity back together. I like that and completely agree with it."

"That's honestly why I helped start all this." David chimed in. "After Jill and Ethan were killed, I saw how horrible the military was and what they stood for and it made me sick."

"How did they die?" Ally asked softly. "If you don't mind me asking." I saw a shadow cross his face in the rearview mirror.

"I was working in the hospital the day the bombs fell," he started. "I had retired from the military years before that, but still had the training, so I became a triage doctor. It was a Saturday; Ethan had an away game across town and Jill had taken him to it. When the sirens went off the military forced a lot of us, doctors and nurses, into the tunnel beneath the hospital that led to the bunker. I was fighting them, telling them that we had to go get my family, they kept telling me that they had to keep us alive, that there wasn't time. I fought on; it took three of them to drag me down into the bunker. As soon as the doors closed, the bombs started falling."

"I was furious," he continued, Mom holding his hand at this point. "I kept fighting them, trying to get out, trying to go save them. Part of me knew it was hopeless, but I didn't care. I was so angry that they didn't even try or wouldn't even let me try to save them. They ended up sedating me for a few days. When they woke me long enough to tell me that they were freezing us, I fought more, screaming at them that they had killed my wife and son. They forced me into the cryotube and froze me anyway." Ally squeezed my hand, I could see tears in her eyes, even I felt sorry for him.

"When they woke me 60 something years later," he said. "I knew I had to get out, but I knew that I would have to bide my time. There were others that had worked in the hospital with me, that had lost their families too because the military refused to help. So, when they let us go top side as we wanted, we started stocking supplies up there. When we had enough to last us some time, we left and never went back. I, of course, went to where Ethan's game had been to try and find out if they had made it to a shelter there. I found their bodies in our car in the parking lot of the stadium."

"I'm so sorry," I said softly. He caught my eye in the mirror and smiled slightly.

"After that, those of us who had lost families because of the military banded together," he continued. "We formed our own family, our own tribe. That's where it all started and of course it grew from there. There's a lot of people who were affected by the military, in one way or another. A lot of people were angry that they were ultimately responsible for the war."

"How long ago was that?" I asked.

"About 12 years now," he said. "Ever since then I've been traveling the world, trying to unite as many people as I can. Spread the word that we all need to stand strong if we're ever going to get the world back to anything like it was before."

"How can we hope to do that?" I asked.

"We out number what's left of the worlds military," he said, matter-of-factly. "We're just so busy fighting each other, that we don't see the power that we have. If we can get enough people on our side, we can take them out and make the world a better place all around."

I sat there, thinking about what he said. It made sense, there's probably not a lot of military left in any country. At least, not a lot that are still siding with old orders. It could be possible to beat them.

"What's the timeline on something like that?" Ally asked and David sighed.

"Unfortunately," he said. "I haven't officially made one. I'm in contact with people all over the world, but coordinating an attack like this takes a lot of man power and planning. We'd have to hit every bunker possible at the same time. We're not sure if the different countries have been in contact with each other, but we can't risk one alerting any others if they are."

"That sounds impossible," I said flatly. David laughed.

"That's what a lot of people tell me," he said lightly. "But I have faith that we can do it. It just takes time to get it organized." Ally rubbed her head, her eyes scrunched in pain.

"You okay?" I asked, squeezing her shoulder. She leaned her head against my chest.

"Just a headache," she said. "I've been getting them a lot lately."

"Maybe you should try and get some sleep, babe," I replied and kissed her forehead. She sighed but snuggled closer to me.

"I guess." I smiled and lightly ran my fingers over her arm, trying to relax her.

The next few days were just a blur of the road and stopping random places for the night. Sometimes we would run into headhunters and David would introduce us all. Other times, we would be on the road for hours without seeing anyone. I noticed Ally rubbing her head a lot more often than before. I was concerned, but she continued to tell me she was fine.

We made it through China and Thailand without an issue. When we got to Malaysia, David was able to get us on a ship for the last leg of our journey. I guess he came in handy after all. I had never been on a ship, at least not the I could remember. I was standing on the deck, leaning against the railing, just watching the water. Part of me was surprised I wasn't seasick.

"There you are," I heard behind me, I turned to see Ally walking towards me. "I was looking for you."

"You found me," I said as I wrapped my arms around her between me and the railing. We stood there a few minutes in silence watching the water. "It's so peaceful out here."

"Yeah it is," she said. "I'm hoping to lay out on the beach when we get there, get a tan." I laughed.

"Is this a nude beach?" I grinned.

"If you're lucky," she said and poked me in the side. I folded and she laughed. She leaned into my chest and I held her tightly. "Are we gonna join the fight?"

"I don't know," I sighed. "Part of me wants to, for all those people that died, for all those people being controlled and lied to now…"

"And the other part?"

"The other part," I started. "Wants to find a secluded area with a beach and just be with you for the rest of my life."

"Hmm," she said thoughtfully. "I can agree with both of those. We still have time to decide. Who knows, maybe we'll get our seclusion and get bored." I laughed.

"That's possible," I agreed. "We'll just play it by ear for now, deal?"

"Deal." I kissed her softly.

After we made it to Australia, we were able to get another car and head further inland, to a tribe David has been to many times. It was only about an hour from when we got off the ship to the tribe. When we pulled in we were met by the usual heavily armed welcome committee. David got out first and talked to them and then nodded to us, we had a routine by now, we all got out. Duke ran off to sniff around and relive himself. We were introduced, small talk, I always found it boring. I was looking around; this was the largest tribe that we've been to so far. It made sense why David wanted us here, safety in numbers.

The first night was eventful, lots of talking and laughing, getting to know each other. Dinner was filled with chatter and adventure stories. Ally fit in well, as usual, with me by her side, just enjoying the almost peace. After almost two weeks of traveling, we had made it. We were safe, at least that's what Ally kept telling me. Part of me was skeptical, but Ally pointed out that I was always skeptical.

We were shown our room, in an old hotel. Mom went off with David to their room, which I had gotten used to, mostly. Ally and I crawled into bed and fell asleep easily. Duke asleep on the floor beside our bed.

I woke up some hours later and was alone in bed. I sat up, automatically in panic mode, but saw the light in the bathroom. I calmed a bit and stood up, walking over to the door. I heard crying.

"Ally?" I said softly, pushing the door open all the way. Ally was sitting on the edge of the tub, wrapped in a towel, hair wet, and had both hands on either side of her head. Her eyes were closed, and she was crying softly. Duke was sitting in front of her, looking worried. I knelt in front of her and placed my hands over hers. "What's wrong Ally?" She jumped slightly at my touch and looked at me. I could see the pain in her eyes.

"My head," she whispered. "It's pounding. I can't stop it. It hurts so much." She cried harder and threw her arms around my neck. I squeezed her tightly.

"It's okay, baby," I whispered softly, afraid of making too much noise. "David said they have other doctors here, equipment, medicine. Maybe they can help."

"It's too early to wake everyone up," she said.

"Come on," I said, standing and picking her up in my arms. "Let's go lay down and we'll get you checked out first thing in the morning. I promise." I walked back to the bed and laid her down, sitting down close to her head. I softly rubbed her temples, trying to ease her pain. She wrapped herself around my legs and groaned.

"It's okay, baby," I said softly. "We'll get you taken care of. I'll take care of you."

She finally fell asleep again after a while, but I was too stressed to sleep again. I laid beside her, my arms around her, worried that this could be worse than the doctors here could handle.

I must have fallen asleep again, because I awoke to a knock at the door. Luckily, it didn't wake Ally. I slipped out of bed, making sure not to wake her and went to the door. Mom was standing on the other side.

"We've got breakfast going down—" she stopped when she saw my face. "What's wrong?" I stepped out in the hall and shut the door behind me. Duke bolted down the hall, probably to go outside.

"Ally," I started. "Her headaches are getting worse. I'm worried it might be something more serious. David said there were other doctors here?"

"Yes," Mom said. "I'll go talk to him. Do you want to bring her downstairs or have him come up here?"

"I think she'll be okay coming downstairs," I said, looking back at the door. "She's still asleep but let me talk to her and find out. Talk to David and see what he can set up for her." Mom nodded and squeezed my arm.

"She'll be okay, honey," she said, before turning and walking down the hall. I opened the door again and stepped inside. Ally was awake, sitting up and looked at me when I came in. I closed to door behind me and went to sit next to her.

"How are you feeling?" I asked, brushing the hair away from her face. She sighed.

"It still hurts," she said. "But less than last night."

"Mom's gonna talk to David and see what we can get set up to figure out what's going on okay?" she nodded. "You wanna get dressed? As much as I love the look, I'd like to keep it for myself." She looked down and laughed, she was still naked, with just the blanket over her.

"If you insist," she said and pulled the blanket off to stand up. I raised an eyebrow and she smirked, shaking her ass as she headed for the table with our stuff on it. "As much as I love messing with you, you have to keep it in your pants. I can't focus on anything right now." I chuckled.

"I wasn't thinking about anything," I said in mock innocence and she laughed. "I'm more worried about you right now."

"I'll survive," she said, getting dressed. "Though how do you feel about a brainless girlfriend? 'Cause we might have to just rip it out you know?"

"Not a chance," I said. "I'm not into zombie chicks, sorry. I like your brain, we're keeping it." She smiled and sat down with me again, fully dressed. She leaned her head into my chest and sighed. I ran my fingers through her hair, trying to calm her and myself at the same time.

"I don't like doctors," she said, muffled by my shirt and her hair.

"You were a nurse," I pointed out.

"Not the same thing," she mumbled. "They tend to be full of themselves. The whole God power thing. I don't know."

"That's fair."

"Will you stay with me through all this?"

"Always." She leaned back and lightly kissed me. I could tell she was scared, so was I.

We walked downstairs, found our way to the dinning room area. I saw Mom and David sitting in the corner with a few other men I remember seeing from dinner the night before. I held Ally's hand and lead the way to their table.

"How are you feeling?" Mom asked as Ally sat beside her and I sat on Ally's other side. Mom squeezed Ally's hand on the table.

"Like my brain is melting?" Ally forced a smile and Mom squeezed her hand again. David leaned across the table.

"Ally," he started. "These are the best doctors we have here." He gestured to three men around the table. "This is Dr. Chase, Dr. Evans, and Dr. Rogers. Dr. Rogers was head of the neurology department in Sydney before the War. We'll get this figured out; I promise." Ally nodded and squeezed my hand under the table.

"Luckily," Dr. Rogers started. "We weren't as affected by the war here, so we do have some equipment. My team and I have been working to make it all operational again, given the long-time frame between uses. But I want to start with an MRI, get an image of your brain and see what's in there."

"Probably a lot of air," Ally said, and I chuckled. The doctors, apparently, were all business.

"When did these headaches start?" Dr. Chase asked, pen and paper in front of him.

"About a week or a week and a half ago," Ally said, thinking. "Not too long after we left the bunker actually." Dr. Chase scratched away at his paper.

"You were in the experiment in there? They wiped your memory?" Dr. Evans asked.

"Yes," she said. "But they took the implant out when they took me out of it. I have all my memories back now."

"And you haven't had any other procedures since then?"

"Not as far as I know."

"Are you thinking that they did something to her?" I asked.

"We don't anything yet, Leo," David said. "But we've been discussing possibilities and the government is a big one. We won't know for sure till we check her out."

"It's going to take us a couple of hours to get the MRI up," Dr. Rogers said, standing up. "Unfortunately, it takes a lot of power, so we have to get some generators in place before we can actually use it. Meet us over there about noon?" I nod and the doctors all leave.

"Is it safe to use on generator power?" Ally asked.

"Yes," David said. "Completely. They've done it many times; it just takes a lot of them to run it properly. Don't worry, they're professionals." He smiled at Ally, who smiled back, though not a true smile. I squeezed her hand again.

"You should eat something," Mom said. "Leo you too. Come on, help me get her some food." I kissed Ally on the cheek and followed my mother.

"She'll be okay," Mom said once we were out of ear shot.

"I know," I said. "I'm just worried."

"David has known these doctors for years. He trusts them and we all know how important Ally is to you," she smiled as we loaded a few plates with food. "He'll help in any way he can."

"I know and I appreciate it."

We headed back to the table and Ally and I picked at our food for a while. Mom and David talked about things around the area, but I wasn't listening. I was thinking and worrying, some of the things I do best. I was terrified that I would lose Ally, after I finally just got her back.

We decided to go for a walk before the MRI. The tribe was definitely more of a town than a tribe. I liked it, it felt homey. They told us that we were welcome to stay here as long as we liked. I could see us growing old here, maybe having children, grandchildren. I had to focus on the positive, for Ally.

Noon finally came around and we headed to the medical center. It was small, but it worked for them. We walked into a room with a hospital bed and the doctors were there.

"Go ahead and change into the gown and then we'll take you to get the MRI," Dr. Rogers said. He gestured to the hospital gown on the bed. "It's magnet based, so make sure you take off everything." Ally nodded and they left, closing the door behind them.

Ally got changed and pulled the gown on, I tied to strings behind her back. And wrapped my arms around her stomach. I kissed her cheek and breathed in her scent.

"Relax," she said softly, her hands over mine.

"I'm supposed to be telling you that," I laughed, and she chuckled.

"I love you," she said.

"I love you. It's just a test," I said. "You're not dying yet. You're gonna die an old lady yelling at me 'cause I let the grandkids get into trouble." She laughed.

"Grandkids huh?" she asked and turned in my arms to face me.

"Maybe." I smiled and she kissed me. There was a knock on the door, and it opened without waiting for a response.

"Ready?" Dr. Rogers asked. Ally nodded and pulled me by my hand towards the door.

CHAPTER 20

After the MRI, the docs took some blood, and sent us back to the hotel, saying that they would come find us with the results. Even after a War and limited people on Earth, we still have to wait for the results. I think it's a doctor superiority complex. Making worried people wait longer. They did give Ally some painkillers though, so she was feeling a little better. We went back to the dinning room and got some lunch before heading back to our room. We laid down and just cuddled. I loved being close to her.

There was a knock at the door a while later. I got up and opened it, Mom and David. I let them in and then sat back on the bed with Ally.

"What's up?" I asked. They both sat at the table across from us.

"It appears," David started, looking at his hands in his lap. "That there is a chip in your head."

"A chip?" I asked. "What kind of chip?"

"We're not sure. It's in your frontal lobe, we're not sure what it does or why it's there, but it's probably the reason for your headaches. We're trying to figure out what kind of chip it is, but the best way to do that would be to take it out."

"Brain surgery?" Ally asked, she looked pale, I squeezed her hand.

"We aren't as well equipped here as they were in the bunker," David said slowly. "But we could do it. We're still looking into other things right now, but ultimately it would be best to take it out. Not only for your headaches, but also for whatever it is doing to you."

"How do we know it's doing anything?" I asked.

"It's active," David said. "It's sending and receiving signals; we just can't pinpoint from where yet. We're working on it. We'd have to run more tests."

"You don't have to decide on this right now," Mom said, cutting in. "Take tonight and think about it. You have the painkillers for the headaches for now. We can talk about it more tomorrow." Ally nodded and I did too after a minute.

"There's something else," David said. "Ally, you're pregnant." I felt my heart stop for a moment.

"Pregnant?" Ally said softly. "You're sure?"

"It's one of the blood tests they gave you, just to be sure," David responded. "You're definitely pregnant though." We were all quiet for a moment. Normally, this would be amazing news, but there was just so much going on, it was almost impossible to have a normal reaction.

"Wow," I said and Ally chuckled a bit.

"We'll talk more in the morning," David said. They left and Ally leaned into me, I put my arms around her, squeezing her tight.

"What do we do?" she asked.

"We're gonna have a baby," I said, confidently. Now that my mind had had time to process the information, I was excited. Ally pulled back and looked at me.

"I meant about the chip in my head," she said and I laughed a little.

"I'm sorry," I said. "Priorities right now."

"Exactly," she said.

"I honestly don't know," I said. "But I don't like the idea of your brain sending and receiving signals from some unknown source."

"Me either," she said. "They're gonna know all my secrets before I do." I chuckled.

"We'll get through this."

"Promise?"

"Promise," I said confidently. "You wanna lay down? Try and get some sleep?" Ally nodded and we laid down, curled together.

"We're gonna have a baby," she whispered and I could hear the smile in her voice. I pulled her closer.

Someone was screaming. Was I dreaming? A memory? No. My eyes snapped open and I immediately saw Ally sitting in the corner of the room, screaming, crying. Her hands clasped on either side of her head. I ran over to her, trying to pull her hands away from her head.

"Ally!" I said loudly. "Ally! Baby, talk to me!"

She was writhing, obviously in pain. I didn't know what to do. I didn't know how to stop it. I was used to fighting things I could see. The door burst open behind me, Mom and David ran inside, both with terrified looks, Duke on their heels. They saw the scene in front of them and understood. Ally stopped screaming for a minute but continued squeezing her head.

"Ally," I said, scared. "Ally talk to me."

"It hurts!" She yelled. She was twitching, like she was getting electrocuted.

"This is different," I said, looking at David who was kneeling next to me. "What is this?"

"This—" a voice said from the door. We all turned to see Ryan standing in the doorway, gun pointed at us. "—Is the end." I stood up quickly, staring at her. Duke growled but stood in front of Ally.

"Ryan?" I asked bewildered. "What is going on? What are you doing here?"

"Well, hello to you too," she sneered. She held up a remote of some kind in her other hand, pointed it at Ally and hit a button. Ally stopped twitching and blinked, like she didn't know what had happened.

"Ally?" I went to her side again. "Are you okay?" She nodded and stood up with my help. Then she saw Ryan in the doorway.

"Ryan?" She asked and then looked back at me. "What's going on?" I shook my head.

"I have no idea," I said, turning to face Ryan, keeping Ally slightly behind me. "Tell me what's going on."

"Always straight to business," She said and shook her head. "You never change, do you?" I glanced at the gun and then the remote in her hand and back at Ally, it clicked.

"You're controlling the chip in her head?" I said, only half questioning.

"Very good," Ryan said, waving the remote in her hand. "This little nifty thing has allowed us to track you since you guys left the bunker. It was a brilliant idea on my part."

"Your part? You did this to her?" I snapped.

"Oh relax, Leo," she said calmly. "Always so high strung. But yes, I have a little more authority than I led you to believe. See I knew that you would want to keep her safe no matter what, and since we knew your mother—" She gestured towards Mom "—was up on the surface waiting for you and that she had been in contact with David here, I knew that he would take you all to his little tribe of headhunters. So, I suggested that we track you and follow you to their little base, so we could take out as many as possible all in one fail swoop. Controlling your little would be girlfriend was just a bonus really."

"But how?" I asked, confused.

"Did you really think it would be that easy to escape?" Ryan asked, sneering. "Think about it Leo. We've had this plan for years. I even spent time watching tapes of you and Ally before you got in the experiment, so I could copy her mannerisms. You obviously have a type." She laughed. "Once I gained your trust in there, we started planning how to pull you out, since Ally was already out. Both of your rooms and bathrooms were monitored after that. We fed you little details and let you play detective for a while."

She hit another button on her remote and Ally got rigid. I turned to look at her, her eyes were terrified, but she didn't say anything.

"Come here Allison," Ryan said and to my surprise, Ally started walking towards her. I grabbed her hand, but Ryan raised her gun at me. "Let her go Leo." I released her. Duke lunged at Ally, biting her hand, trying to pull her back towards me. Ryan stepped forward and shot him without a second's hesitation. I heard a small yelp and Duke lay unmoving on the floor. Ally walked to Ryan and stood slightly behind her. I knelt down next to Duke and tried to find a pulse. There was none, I was furious.

"I'll kill you," I muttered as I stood up again. Ryan had her gun trained on me now.

"So, you've been keeping tabs on me and David?" Mom asked, cutting in. "Why?"

"David we've been tracking for a while," Ryan continued, my eyes were on Ally's the whole time. I could tell whatever this chip was, couldn't control her emotions, just her movements, and apparently her ability to speak. There were tears running down her face. "The whole enemy thing. When he met you and we figured out who you were, we set the whole thing in motion. Putting the chip in the bimbo's brain—" I clenched my fists. "—when we restored her memories, the whole soulmate mix up thing to get you out of the experiment without suspicion. Did you really think that we would let her waltz up to the top floor and see all the stuff she did without us letting it happen? Did you really think the first floor would be so empty when you tried to escape? That we wouldn't chase you after you got over the fence? That we didn't know where your house was? That we didn't have surveillance set up there too? You really are stupider than I thought, Leo." She laughed. The gun still pointed at us. Ally still behind her.

"When did you become so cruel?" I asked, angry.

"Me?" Ryan smirked. "This is who I've always been. That little show in the experiment? All an act. Do you think I deserve an Oscar or what?" She laughed.

"You're just gonna come in here and kill all these people?" David asked. "There's too many, you'll never succeed."

"You think I came here alone?" Ryan laughed. "The whole building is already cleared; they're already starting on the rest of the town. I wanted to take care of you myself." I heard an explosion outside, and my hands grew sweaty. We brought this here, we let them follow us, we're responsible for all these people dying. I felt sick to my stomach.

"This is wrong," I said shakily. I saw the guilt in Ally's eyes. "This isn't your fault. It's theirs." I nod towards Ryan and she glanced back at Ally, seeing the tears. She laughed and rammed her elbow into Ally's nose. Ally doubled over in pain, clutching her face. I went to run to her, but Mom moved first, heading directly for Ryan. Ryan simply pulled the trigger and the sound was deafening as my mother fell to the floor. I felt my heart skip a beat, staring at my motionless mother.

I can hear David yelling on his knees beside me, but I can't understand what he's saying. Partly to the ringing in my ears from the gunshot, the other part was the sound of my heart breaking. I was numb and frozen, apparently the only one who was. David was still shouting with tears in his eyes. Ally was on the floor behind Ryan, hands over her mouth now. I could see the tears and the blood on her face. She caught my eye and I could tell that Ryan's control over her was broken, if only for a moment. Ryan stood, pointing the gun at David with a smirk on her face.

"I'll kill you!" I finally heard David shouting. "I'll kill every last one of you!"

"Oh, please," Ryan said. She rolled her eyes and prepared to fire again. Ally jumped to her feet and grabbed Ryan from behind, pulling her backwards, causing the fired round to hit the ceiling above David.

"RUN!" Ally screamed at me. I took a step towards the door but stopped. I couldn't leave her. Ryan would kill her. Ally had knocked the remote out of Ryan's hand, but was still struggling for the gun. "You both have to go! Now!"

David was on his feet grabbing my arm, pulling me towards the door. I struggled against him, but he held tight.

"We can't leave her!" I yelled, still watching the girls struggle. Ryan punched Ally in the stomach and somehow managed to get on top of her. David had pulled me to the door. We just stepped over the threshold when Ally's eyes met mine again. Ryan was on top of her with the gun pointed at her head.

"I love you," she said, and I lost sight of her as David pulled me into the hallway. I heard the shot and my heart shattered completely.

"NO!" I screamed and struggled harder against David. He grabbed me tighter as I tried to get back to the doorway. "ALLY! NO!"

"We have to go!" David said urgently, having to put his arm around my neck as I continued to try and break free of his grasp.

"We have to."

"No!" I yelled. "We have to save Ally! We have to get Mom! We have to—" David pushed me through the door to the stairs.

"We can't do anything now," David said grimly. I could see the streaks on his face from tears, but he stood firm. "We have to leave, before they get us too."

"No—"

"Leo," he cut me off. "Trust me. I want to get these guys as much as you do, but we can't do that if we're dead. We have to leave. If I have to, I'll knock you out and carry you, but we're leaving. Now."

I knew he was right; we couldn't do anything else here without getting killed. I didn't care, my mother and the love of my life were in that room with that murderous bitch. I was going back for them. I ducked around him to get back to the hallway, but he caught me around the neck, choking me.

"I'm sorry, Leo," he said quietly as everything faded to black.

I woke up later in the passenger seat of a car. My head hurt and I was groggy, but I looked over and saw David at the wheel. I couldn't see anything in front of us, just the road and some trees. It was still dark out. I turned to look behind us and couldn't see anything but darkness. Everything came rushing back to me. Duke. Ally. Mom. Ryan. I turned back to David.

"We have to go back," I said flatly, anger rising.

"No," he said, still watching the road. "They've killed or captured everyone; they were setting everything on fire when we left. We barely got out of there alive, we can't do anything against that many of them."

"I don't care! We have to do something! We have to—have to—" I broke down in tears. Mom was gone. Ally was gone. Even Duke was gone. I couldn't handle this. David reached over to grab my shoulder, but I jerked away from him.

"Don't touch me!" I screamed. "Pull over. Now."

"We're not going back."

"I just have to get out of here right now," I snapped, reaching for the door handle. David realized I was gonna jump out and pulled over quickly. I got out of the car and paced back and forth next to it. David got out and stood next to the car, watching me.

"Leo—" He started.

"Shut up!" I screamed. "This is your fault. We could have saved Ally. Maybe Mom. We could have killed Ryan."

"Either she would have killed both of us, or her men would have," David said, trying to keep his voice steady. I could tell that he was just as upset as I was, but he was trying to be the rational one. It made me angrier.

"No!" I lunged at him and tackled him into the car. He didn't try to stop me at all, which fueled my anger more. I reared back and punched him in the face. He hit the ground, face down. I rolled him over and straddled him, punching him in the face, over and over again. "This. Is. Your. Fault." Every word followed by a punch. "I'll. Kill. You." My arm started to get tired, the punches slowed.

"You can't kill me," David said with blood in his mouth, cuts all along his face. "I already died back in that hotel room." My arm stopped, still poised for another punch. His words finally sunk in and my hand dropped to my side. I got off of him and sat on the ground with my back against the car. My head in my hands, letting the tears fall again. I heard David moving, spitting blood from his mouth, but I didn't look at him.

We sat there in silence for a long while, both crying, both dealing with our losses. I cried until I was numb, and no more tears would come. I finally lifted my head and looked at David. The entire left side of his face was bloody and swollen. His left eye was totally swollen shut. Bruises already showing were there wasn't blood. I felt terrible.

"I'm sorry," I whispered, and he chuckled dryly.

"It's okay," he said. "I had it coming."

"No. You got us out. We would both be dead if you wouldn't have gotten us out," I said and stared out in space.

"We'll get them, Leo. I promise you; we'll beat them."

"No," I said, determined now. For Ally. For my unborn baby. For Mom. For Duke. For everyone that has ever been hurt by them. For everyone who has been killed by them. "I'm going to do more than that."

"What do you mean?" he asked, a look of confusion on his face.

"I'm going to kill them all."

We found a small house to sleep in for the night, but it was short lived. They found us before the sun came up. Without Duke and his advanced hearing, we didn't hear them until they were already inside. I woke to them rolling me onto my stomach. I reached for the pistol under my pillow, but it was wrenched from my grasp before I could shoot any of them. They pulled my hands behind my back and zip tied my wrists together. David was on his knees beside me, his hands bound as well.

"Well that was a fun chase," Balding Joe and Ryan had walked in, after the soldiers had us under control. I glared.

"I'll kill you," I snapped.

"Don't speak to my father like that," Ryan sneered, pressing the barrel of her pistol into my forehead.

"Your father?" I asked, unable to hide my surprise.

"Yes," Joe said simply. "Ryan is my daughter and she's been with me on all of this from the beginning."

"Well that explains a lot," I said bitterly.

"I really expected more from you, Leo," Ryan said. "I mean I did just kill your dog, your mom, your girlfriend and your unborn baby." She ticked them off on her fingers like she was listing groceries she needed to buy. I lunged and screamed at her trying to reach her. I'd bite her eyes out if I could get to her. The soldiers held my arms denying me my revenge.

"Fuck you," I said, coldly.

"There's that temper," Joe said.

"Why don't you just kill us already?" David asked suddenly.

"We could," Ryan mused. "Or you could always join us. With your military background and leadership, you could be a general in no time, David."

"I'd rather die than join you," David spat at her.

"Your wish is my command," Ryan said simply. She pressed the barrel of her pistol to David's forehead and pulled the trigger. David slumped over and I screamed.

"What about you, Leo?" Joe asked, in his sickly calm voice. "Should we kill you too?"

"You can't kill me. I already died back in that hotel room," I said, repeating David's words to me.

"We'll see," Ryan said, I closed my eyes and pictured Ally's face. At least I would finally see her again. I heard the shot and there was darkness.

CHAPTER 21

There was a bright light in my eyes and part of me wondered if this was heaven. Then the light moved and there was a face looking at me. I jerked backwards, but hands grabbed my shoulders and wrists.

"It's okay, soldier," the man with the flashlight said. "Relax, you're safe."

"Where's Ally?" I asked, automatically, before remembering she was dead.

"Who's Ally?" the man asked.

"What?" I stopped struggling and stared at him.

"You're going to be disoriented," the man said. "But it's going to be okay, James."

"Who's James?" I snapped. The people around me looked at each other.

"You…" The man holding my shoulder started. "You are James."

"My name is Leo Parks," I said loudly and struggled to get away from them again.

"Sedate him," one of them said and I felt a needle prick.

I woke again later, strapped to a bed. I couldn't move at all but yelled until someone came into the room.

"Where am I?" I asked. "Who are you people?"

"Hello," The woman said simply and sat in the chair near the foot of my bed. "My name is Dr. Granger. You are in a psychiatric facility in Los Angeles, California." I stared at her and then noticed the green trees outside my window. LA should have been bombed in the war, there's no way it recovered that quickly.

"Where am I really?" I snapped and she tilted her head.

"I'm afraid I don't understand," she said calmly.

"The trees," I said. "LA was bombed in the war, there's no way that there's trees in LA now. So where am I really?"

"What war are you talking about?" she asked and I was getting irritated.

"World War III," I snapped. "Everyone released nukes and it wiped out most of the world. I'm not an idiot."

"What year do you think it is?" she asked, still calm. She reminded me of Balding Joe and Ryan and part of me was wondering if she worked for them. But what would be the point of making me think I'm crazy? There's no motivation for that.

"What are you talking about?" I said sharply. "It's 2122."

"I see," she said. She pulled a pen and notepad from somewhere and began writing. "And what is your name?"

"Leo Parks," I said. "You want to explain to me what is going on and why I'm here, wherever here is?"

"I don't have the clearance to tell you what happened," She said, still writing. "But I will see if I can get someone in here who does. How does that sound?" She stood and patted my foot before leaving the room.

She was treating me like I was crazy, or a child. It was infuriating, I still couldn't move, but could still see the trees outside.

They were swaying in the breeze, it was daytime, but must have been cloudy. That is, if that wasn't a projection or something.

I thought that this had to be something set up by Ryan and Joe, but it didn't make sense. She had shot me in the head, at close range. I should be dead. Like Duke, and Ally, and Mom and David. None of this made sense. What is this place? Just a figment of my imagination? But why would I imagine myself in a psychiatric hospital?

I don't know how much time had passed, there was no clock or anything in my room, but the next time the door opened, Dr. Granger was back with an official looking man.

"Are you the one who's supposed to tell me what's going on?" I asked, sarcastically.

"My name is Dr. Robert Walker," he said. "And I can tell you what happened, but not necessarily what is currently happening. You were part of an experiment with the military—"

"I know," I snapped. "We were underground, and it was about fertility and we escaped and blah blah blah."

"No," he started. "Let me start over. Your name is James Martin. You joined the military when you turned 18. After basic training and a few tours, you volunteered for a project dedicated to seeing how people would handle being in a post-apocalyptic world. The project involved you being put into a coma-like state. We would feed certain stipulations in regard to conditions of the world in your mind. Like World War III and nuclear war and fallout shelters. We allowed your own mind to fill in the rest of the details. Though none of subjects took it quite as far as you did. I assume it has something to do with growing up in foster care all through your childhood, but that's neither here nor there—"

"Wait," I said. I had remained silent through this, mostly from shock, but I finally found my voice again. "What year are you saying it is?"

"Today's date is May 25th, 2048," he said with a glance at his watch.

"And what did you say my name was?" I asked.

"James Martin," he replied.

"So, you're saying that I made everything up?" I asked. "My name? My parents? The love of my life? Our unborn child? The whole bunker with the experiment? Everything?"

"Yes," he said. "As I said, you took it farther than any of our other subjects." I laughed and both he and Dr. Granger looked shocked. I laughed harder.

"You're kidding right?" I said, still laughing. "I made everything up? You said I was in foster care? So let me guess my parents died when I was little? Or was it that I got abandoned when I was a baby?"

"You were left at a fire house when you were—"

"BULLSHIT!" I bellowed and they both jumped. "My parents names were Carolyn and Matthew Parks. I lived with them until the sirens went off and Allison Sherrow and I went into the bunker to avoid the bombs and then they froze everyone for 60 or so years. We woke up and they were doing an experiment to try and deal with the fertility issues due to the radiation from the War." They both just stared at me. "You guys think I'm crazy, don't you? I remember it all."

"We never said you were crazy," Dr. Granger said calmly. "We just think there's some issues with letting go of what you want your life to be versus what it actually is, James."

"MY NAME IS LEO!" I yelled again and they jumped. "Get out. I'm not crazy. I don't want to talk to you people anymore."

They slowly stood and left my room. I laid there staring at the ceiling for a while, thinking about everything that they had said. James didn't sound familiar to me at all. You would think, if it was my name that there would be some familiarity, but there was nothing. My name was Leo. James just sounded wrong. And the whole thing about me being left at a fire house? That can't be right either. I remember my parents. I remember talking to them and hugging them and loving them. They're real. I didn't grow up in foster care. It was all lies. They were the crazy ones.

I slept, but not well. I kept watching their deaths in replay. Watching Ryan kill everyone I cared about. I woke up sweating and crying more than once. They still hadn't removed my binds. Still convinced I was crazy and had some sort of psychotic break or something. It was hard enough to sleep with the nightmares, let alone not being able to move much. Sometimes I just laid there and pictured Ally's face in my mind. I thought about what we would have named our baby. Sometimes I even pictured her sitting in the chair in my room, talking to me, telling me everything was going to be alright.

"Do you think he'll ever come out of it?" Dr. Walker asked Dr. Granger. They stood outside James Martin's room, watching him speak to someone only he could see.

"I don't know," Dr. Granger responded. "It's been a week and it just seems to be getting worse. He's convinced that he's speaking to this woman 'Ally.' The one who is supposedly dead, but he changes the subject when I ask how she could be here if she died."

"Hmm," he said. "I was hoping it would improve with time. He was an amazing soldier, we had high hopes for him."

"There's still hope of course," she said. "There's always a chance that a certain medication will help or that he'll just somehow snap out of it one day. Anything is possible. We're keeping our spirits high around here."

"I hope you're right," he said, still watching James speak to this invisible Ally woman. He felt sorry for him. He sighed heavily. "Keep me informed if there's any progress."

"Yes, sir," she said and Dr. Walker walked away. Dr. Granger stood watching James for a minute more, saw his lips form the words 'I love you' to his invisible girlfriend, then she too sighed and walked away.

ABOUT THE AUTHOR

Weylyn Benson

As a child I experienced many family struggles. My stories were a way to get through those tough times. At the age of 12 I began writing them down to make room for even more stories. They allowed me to have an escape. To have reality as I chose and wanted it to be. After many years of self-doubt, the courage to publish came through and I wanted to share my stories to help others get through their own life struggles. I hope my stories can be that escape for other people.

Author Photo By: Michelle Lynn

Made in the USA
Monee, IL
23 July 2021